LAST MAN HOME

THE FINAL BOOK IN THE
LMF TRILOGY

MALCOLM HAVARD

Oakbrook Press

Oakbrook Press

LAST MAN HOME

PROLOGUE

(From The Way Back) - June 5th, 1944

Dag tried to keep his breathing steady and as quiet as possible. At least the warmth of the day ensured his breath did not fog, as it was, he had to be almost silent as the searchers were now awfully close.

He had heard them for the last twenty minutes, the voices, the shouts, the occasional bark of dogs. They must be convinced that C-Charlie had been crewed when it crashed; he'd obviously done too good a job getting the old chap down, yes, it was smashed and burning when it had slid to a halt, but it was obviously under control before the crash, hence the search parties.

Well, he'd got away before they'd arrived, avoided the obvious temptation afforded by the farm buildings he'd found but had followed one of the thick hedgerows away from the roads and buildings. At first light he'd started to look for a lair where he could lie low until things had died down. He'd found it under one of the hedges, a way in, low to the ground where, inside, there was a natural hollow under the branches. He could stay there hidden from view for as long as he needed.

He hadn't counted on dogs though.

If the party that was making its way closer and closer to him had a dog with him, he would be caught. He'd probably be fine if he was. They might hand him over Gestapo if they suspected he was part of the drop but, surely, he'd end up in a POW camp eventually.

But he'd rather not. Dag was determined to evade, to make it back home. Back to Blighty. Back to Bette.

Not if they had dogs. They were here now, alongside the hedge. No dogs. The men were laughing, joking. They sounded relaxed, just going through the motions most likely. If they weren't so close, he would have breathed a sigh of relief. He couldn't understand their words but whatever the language, this sounded very much like a bunch of lads who'd been ordered to look for someone who they didn't expect to find. That suited Dag perfectly.

They soon passed, their voices fading away. Dag now did sigh in relief. He checked his watch; just after 3pm. He'd move at dusk. A long while yet. He might as well try to sleep. He wondered where Faz and the boys were. Had they managed to evade too? They would have bailed out closer to the resistance, maybe they would have been able to meet up. Maybe they were prisoners now.

He couldn't know.

Be nice to see them again though. Have a pint or three with them.

***

Dag had made good progress since he had eased his stiff and sore body out from under the hedge as the evening drew in, though things had slowed down now it was fully dark.

The clouds were thick. There being little moonlight had its advantages; he would be harder to spot but it was also more difficult to find his way through the fields. He tried to keep away from the roads, but it was proving virtually impossible to find ways through the thick hedgerows and built-up banks that surrounded each field. After tripping several times, he decided he had no choice; he would have to risk it on a road.

It was midnight by the time he managed to find one and then only because a vehicle drove down it. Although its lights were masked against the blackout, it was still clear enough for him to work out where he needed to head, and it took another twenty minutes for him to find a way out of the field. Now he was there he needed to decide which direction to head. He consulted the tiny compass he had retrieved from his boot, part of the standard escape kit all crew carried. The luminous pointer told him that the road was running virtually north/south. South was towards the hinterland of France. Most of the canisters and agents he'd delivered to had been in that direction. North was the coast, heavily defended, Hitler's much vaunted Atlantic wall. There'd be more troops that way, much more chance of being caught.

He was still trying to decide when he heard it; the drone of aeroengines, a lot of them. To the north flak rose into the sky, first a few streaks then a veritable barrage. They were joined by searchlights. Soon the unmistakable heavy concussion of bombs was added to the cacophony. A raid. And not just one. To the right and left of the original flak more opened up. The sky seemed to be filled with aircraft. Something big was happening, something in the North. That would be the Normandy coast. Invasion? It was worth a try. This could be the most dangerous place on earth to be right now, but this could also be his best chance of getting back.

Dag set off along the road, heading North.

Fifteen minutes later, with the virtual fireworks still going off, Dag suddenly smelt something. It was blowing in from one of the fields to the side, the reek of high-octane aviation fuel and the smell of burning. An aircraft had crashed and burned somewhere near where he was, and recently. Who's though? A Yank crate, or a RAF machine. Or a Jerry?

There was one machine he did know had crashed and burned near here - his own C-Charlie.

It couldn't be, could it? Actually, he decided, it could be and probably was. When he'd extricated himself from the smashed cockpit, going out of the split in the rear where the Halifax had, as per usual, come apart on impact, he'd not cared what direction he'd run off in. He was sure the Jerries would quickly find the burning wreck, so he wasn't going to hang around and get caught. He could well have circled around again and was now back at the wreck site.

Walking a little further down the road, his supposition was confirmed. The pyrotechnic show revealed a gap had been made in the hedge, possibly by a bulldozer or tank, and wheel tracks could be seen heading out across the field. At the entrance some piled up debris had been discarded. It was aluminium, painted black. One bit had part of a serial number on it written in the typical RAF night bomber dull red. It was Charlies' serial number.

That was probably what the Germans were after, Dag decided, an identity for the machine, to see if they could place it in a unit. He was sure that RAF intelligence would do the same if this were a German aircraft. He paused looking towards the place where Charlies' flying days had come to an end.

'Poor old girl,' he muttered. Suddenly the ground was illuminated by a brilliant light in the sky, so bright it was almost like the sun had risen: a parachute flare. Whether this had been dropped by a raiding aircraft or fired from the ground didn't matter; Dag was now incredibly vulnerable, anyone nearby would see him straightaway.

He dived off the road and into the field, hiding behind the hedge. But was that safe? What if there were guards around the wreck, they were sure to see him. Dag pushed himself into the ground but lifted his head to scan the crash site. No, he was fine.

Cautiously he pushed himself to his feet.

Then stared in horror. Not twenty feet away, clearly visible in the light of the now fading flare was an area of disturbed ground, close to the field entry but away from the main track leading to the wreckage.

There could be no doubt about what they were.

Graves. Makeshift ones, but graves, nonetheless.

Five of them.

He looked again at the burned out remains of C-Charlie.

'No,' he said. 'No, you got out. You had to have. I gave the order. I gave you time.'

Unless, he thought, unless the RT was u/s. Unless they hadn't heard.

'No, no, no, please, no!'

The parachute flare gave one last flash then went out. And with it went Dag's hope.

He knew.

And he knew whose fault it was.

6.20 PM LONDON TELEX OHMS 80

PRIORITY GENERAL A.S. GRIEVE, HARCROFT HOUSE, BALCOMBE STREET, W4

FROM AIR MINISTRY 77 OXFORD ST WI. 12.7.44. DEEPLY REGRET TO INFORM YOU THAT ACCORDING TO INFORMATION RECEIVED FROM COMMANDING OFFICER YOUR SON F/ SGT DOUGLAS ATKINSON-GRIEVE BELIEVED TO HAVE LOST HIS LIFE AS THE RESULT OF AIR OPERATIONS ON NIGHT OF 4/5th /6/44 STOP. THE AIR COUNCIL EXPRESS THEIR PROFOUND SYMPATHY STOP LETTER FOLLOWS SHORTLY STOP

UNDER SECRETARY OF STATE STOP 1512 ATH

YORKSHIRE; FEBRUARY 1951

The applause was polite but unenthusiastic—not unexpected for Bette Baxter, who had grown used to such receptions during her decade in the RAF, a service still dominated by men. The commanding officer tried to extend the applause but quickly gave up.

'Thank you, Squadron-Leader Baxter, for an interesting talk,' he said, inviting questions from the audience. Scanning the crowd, he noticed Flight-Lieutenant Hitchcock raising his hand. Bette reflected that, though the planes were similar to those used in wartime, much had changed since then —perhaps not for the better.

Bette shielded her eyes from the lights as she concentrated on the pilot seated in the second row —a quintessential RAF officer in his mid-twenties, hair approaching regulation limits, and distinguished by a prominent handlebar moustache. She was well-acquainted with the type and surmised he would be confident.

'Thank you, sir,' Hitchcock responded. 'Squadron Leader, with respect, I appreciate your intentions, but I struggle to see how all these additional devices and technical equipment being loaded onto our aircraft are relevant to our operations. They appear to introduce further complications and unnecessary weight. Ultimately, traditional piloting skills and determination secure victory, not this, er, stuff.'

Bette allowed herself a brief smile, recognising his restraint and aware of harsher sentiments previously expressed. Nevertheless, his Commanding Officer intervened in her defence.

'Now, Hitchcock, that's inappropriate. Squadron Leader Baxter is highly regarded—'

'That's quite all right, Wing Commander,' Bette interjected. 'It's a reasonable question and I'm happy to address it.' She turned to Hitchcock. 'I assume you did not serve in the previous war?'

'With respect, ma'am, I'm not that old,' he replied, prompting quiet laughter from his peers.

'Perhaps not, but you are senior to those who filled these seats during my last visit to this room in 1944. If I am correct, you are twenty-five?'

'I'm twenty-six, sir.'

Bette nodded. 'As I thought. Most of the men who occupied your position were between eighteen and twenty-two years old; they had only just finished school. Their lives should have been progressing through university, work placements, or apprenticeships, yet instead, they found themselves flying over occupied Europe under constant threat. Many faced even greater dangers in support of the invasion of France. Tragically, too many never returned to continue building their lives; yet, in some respects, those individuals were considered the fortunate ones.'

'Lucky? Certainly. They were fortunate not to have been flying their missions in 1942, 1943, or even earlier in 1944. The reason for this lies in the advancements made at the Telecommunications Research Establishment which I had, at the time, a small but important role at. Permit me to mention several code names—Tinsel, Cigar, Airborne Cigar, and Jostle—which may sound whimsical but represented significant electronic countermeasures. These systems effectively disrupted radar operations and interfered with controllers' efforts to direct night fighters toward the bomber stream.

On D-Day, these techniques became even more sophisticated; by combining Window with precise flying and strategic radar interference, we successfully misled German forces into believing an invasion fleet was heading for the Pas-de-Calais, while the actual assault targeted Normandy. Many of the young airmen present in this room on June 5th, 1944, owed their survival in subsequent days to these concerted efforts that diverted enemy fighters.

Turning her attention to Hitchcock, she remarked,

'Should you prefer, Flight-Lieutenant, all such equipment can be removed from your aircraft if, unfortunately, you find yourself in combat. However, I suspect your crew might hold a different opinion.' This elicited increased laughter among the group.

Although Bette recognized her effectiveness in engaging such audiences, she felt a persistent sense of unease —a sentiment that had lingered for seven years. Her gaze shifted to an officer wearing freshly sewn squadron leader stripes, a subtle sign visible in the fabric's colour. She sensed familiarity, possibly from past encounters common in long service, yet there was something distinct about his presence. He seemed old enough to have served during the war. It was plausible their paths had crossed before.

Despite her effort, she could not recall exactly where she knew him from. Given the numerous individuals she had met over the years—many of whom had not survived—this was not unexpected. The memory of Dag remained strong among those countless young men who would never grow older.

***

'I enjoyed your talk, Squadron Leader Baxter. But then I would, it's right down my alley.'

Bette wasn't surprised to find it was the officer she'd thought she'd recognised who'd come over to chat in the mess, drink in hand.

'Thank you, and please call me Bette. We are the same rank after all.'

He smiled and self-consciously touched the stripes on his sleeves as if he was checking they were still there. 'We are indeed, now at least. I only got these a couple of weeks ago.' He held out his hand. 'John Hinton. I'm the squadron's radar man, hence my interest.'

'I see, yes.' She frowned, Hinton. Did she know him? 'Excuse me, have we met before? You look familiar.'

He nodded. 'You've got a good memory, Bette, though I was a lowly sprog sparky then and, if memory serves me right you were a Section-leader with a rather mysterious job.' He grinned. 'And now I have an inkling of what that job was.'

She remembered. 'I think I do remember you. You flew Halifaxes, didn't you?'

Hinton nodded. 'I did. Mark IIIs mainly though my

first mission was in a Mark IIa. It was quite the baptism of fire.'

The haze in Bette's memory cleared. Now she knew for certain. 'You flew with Dag.'

He nodded. 'Just the once, yes. That was in that clapped out IIa. It was a damned disgrace what they did to him.'

'It was, yes.' Bette felt the familiar pang of loss. She should move the conversation onto another topic; and quickly. 'Which radar fittings do your kites carry?'

Hinton was frowning, not listening. It seemed he too was trying to remember. 'Weren't you and him walking out together?'

Hell, why couldn't he just leave it? Still, there was no reason not to be pleasant. 'That's a quaint way of putting it. Yes, we were.'

'You didn't stay together after the war then?'

Bette frowned. 'No. That wasn't possible, was it?'

'Shame. Mind you, I imagine life with Dag would have been difficult. Still, he was a good egg.'

'Yes, he was, but –' She braced herself to utter the words; you do know Dag is dead, don't you, but never got the chance.

'It was good to see that he got through it and had a decent life after it.'

'Yes.' She frowned. What had he just said? 'Pardon? What was that?'

'About the radar? Well, I –'

'No, before.'

'About Dag? I was saying it was good to see he got back in the pilot's seat again.'

'Yes, but that didn't last long, did it?'

John frowned. 'It was several years. In fact, I presume he's still doing it. It didn't look like he was any mood to change career. He was quite happy with what he was doing even if it was just a civvie outfit. He was born to fly.'

She stared at him for a few moments then shook her head. 'John, I'm sorry, you must be getting mixed up. Dag is dead. He was lost just before D-Day on a Special Duties mission. Him and all his crew, including the agents they were dropping.'

Now it was John's turn to look puzzled. 'Special duties? Agent dropping? No, that can't be right? Not after, well, you know. They never allowed you to come back from that.'

Even after all the years since the war, John could not

bring himself to utter the dreaded initials: LMF.

Lack of Moral Fibre.

Coward. Failure. Scum of the Earth. Someone who needed to be made an example of.

'It's a long story,' muttered Bette. 'But, believe me, it happened.'

'Fair enough. I suppose Dag always found a way.'

'He did. But he was definitely killed. I was there when the notification came through.'

'Well, that must have been a mistake,' said John. 'It wasn't unknown back then. I knew of a pilot who'd been reported –'

'John, tell me about that later. Why do you think Dag is alive?'

'Easy: I met Dag in France at the opening of the British cemetery at Bayeaux last year. He most definitely wasn't a ghost. He wasn't as pretty as he used to be, but it was him for sure. I had a damned good night with him talking about the old times. Our paths had crossed too though I never knew it. He flew Dakotas into Berlin during the airlift and all that time I was based at Gatow. Anyway, about your talk...' He stopped. 'I say are you all right?'

Bette staggered and swayed. She'd gone suddenly light-headed. It took a few moments to recover and even then, she barely listened to what John was saying.

She was planning a trip.

A trip which would involve asking some awkward questions.

SURREY,
MARCH 1951

It had threatened rain the whole way from London, and by the time Bette stepped off the train, a fine drizzle had begun to settle over the suburban streets. She walked through the hush of neat, leafy avenues—each house a mirror of its neighbour, their gardens raw and unfinished, as if they too were waiting to grow into something better.

Everything here was new: clean brickwork, shining windows, and the subtle, insistent optimism of post-war Britain. It was the kind of neighbourhood you'd find on a Labour Party leaflet: the promise of the National Health Service, nationalised industries, and a future built on hope. Yet, for Bette, all of it felt strangely remote, as if the world's fresh beginnings were passing her by. Britain still wore its austerity like an old coat—ration books, shortages, quiet resolve—but here was a place that seemed determined to believe in better days.

She paused at the gate of one house, her resolve faltering. A tricycle lay on a patch of grass too thin to be called a lawn, and a sandpit, garnished with a scarlet spade and battered bucket, bore the marks of small, determined hands. So, they had children—unsurprising, really, after a 1946 wedding and the abrupt shift from uniform to civilian life. She hadn't known, but perhaps she'd never truly wanted to.

For a moment, she considered leaving, simply retracing her steps and vanishing back into the drizzle. But then a figure appeared at the window: blonde still, though the old film-star glamour had yielded to a practical cut, a style shaped by the weight of a baby on her hip. Recognition flickered across Connie's face—first shock, then a smile, brittle but not unkind. Bette's chance to escape had disappeared.

She pushed open the gate and made her way to the door, which swung open before she could knock.

'Bette. What on earth are you doing here?'

Bette looked at the infant in Connie's arms, then at the toddler peering out from behind his mother's knees—both unmistakable echoes of their parents.

'Hello, Connie,' she said quietly. 'Seems you and Roland have been busy since we last met.'

***

Bette perched uneasily on the edge of the sofa, her presence in this house as ill-fitting as a borrowed coat. What, truly, had possessed her to come? Connie had once been Dag's girl, before Roland and before the shifting tides of war had rearranged them all. The old betrayals—Connie to Roland, Dag left floundering—had been just another fracture in a time already riddled with loss. For Bette, the memory of those days had never truly faded, even as they thinned and frayed around the edges. Connie, though, had become a catalyst, a necessary antagonist who'd helped drive Dag back to the airfields. That, if nothing else, remained an unspoken bone of contention and link between them.

Now she was stranded in a living room littered with the detritus of family life, left alone with a small boy whose sticky hands and perpetual cough made her skin crawl with an unfamiliar blend of guilt and discomfort. The child—Charlie—was engrossed in stacking wooden blocks, jabbering to himself in a private language of shrieks and mutters, the occasional sharp 'No!' punctuating the silence each time his structure collapsed.

Bette considered intervening but hesitated; the boy seemed equal parts fragile and feral. She'd never wanted children—never pictured herself in a room like this, managing tantrums and coughs and the endless clutter of small lives. Still, in some alternate universe, she supposed, this scene might have been hers.

Connie returned from the kitchen, bearing a tray laden with a teapot, delicate willow-patterned China, and a mismatched milk jug. She placed it carefully on the low table.

'I forgot the sugar,' she muttered, already turning

away.

'It's fine, I—' Bette began, but Connie was gone.

She's nervous, Bette thought, watching Connie vanish into the kitchen. Was it Bette's presence, dredging up all those years, or was there something more behind the tightly drawn mouth and restless hands?

When Connie returned, she perched on the armchair as if poised for flight, twisting a handkerchief between her fingers, eyes fixed on anything but Bette.

'No! No! Nooooo!' Charlie howled as his latest tower collapsed spectacularly.

'Play nicely, Charlie,' Connie called wearily. 'You'll wake your sister. Please, I've only just got her down.'

'Hate bay, hate bay,' the boy shrieked, flinging a block across the room. It clipped Bette's shoulder.

'Enough. Bed for you,' Connie announced, scooping him up. Charlie protested in escalating waves of 'Not tired, not, not not!' as she carried him upstairs.

Alone again, Bette surveyed the wreckage of the room. For want of something to do, she poured the tea, then hesitated—was it right to pour for Connie? She placed the saucer over Connie's cup, a small, practical gesture meant to keep it warm.

By the time Connie returned, Bette had finished one cup and was halfway through her second. Connie reclaimed her seat, the handkerchief gone, perhaps abandoned mid-crisis. Charlie's cries drifted down from above, gradually subsiding.

'He'll sleep soon,' Connie offered, unnecessarily.

'You look tired.'

'Thanks,' Connie replied, sharper than intended. 'I hadn't noticed.'

This is going well, Bette thought. She'd try a different path, one where the ice might be thicker.

'How's Roland? What's he doing now?'

'He's an accountant. He's doing well, works in the city.'

'A bit of a change from the RAF.'

'Of course. That's all ancient history now, isn't it, best forgotten.'

Bette shrugged. 'Not for me. I stayed on.'

'We didn't, Roland and I, did we? The war was over; we'd done our bit.' Connie's voice was suddenly cold. 'Why are you here, Bette? It's obviously not to ask about our health, is it? I mean, it's not as if we ever knew each other that well, is it? Nor got on particularly well.'

'No.' Bette placed her cup on the coffee table. 'You must have guessed why I'm here?'

Connie pulled a face. 'Dag? He's the only thing we had in common.'

'We had a career in common, Connie.'

'Not anymore. So, it is Dag, isn't it? What about him? Can't you leave him alone? Haven't you done enough to him?'

Bette stared at Connie. 'Enough? What did I do?'

Connie was on her feet. 'I think you'd better go, Bette.' She pointed at the door.

Bette rose too. 'Connie, I didn't mean to upset you? And as for Dag...' She paused, thinking. 'Wait, you said, 'Can't you leave him alone?"

'Yes, why can't you?'

'You used the present tense.'

Connie hesitated, then recovered.

'So? I misspoke. What of it?'

'He's alive, isn't he?'

Connie distinctly reddened. 'Of course not, he died in France, on D-Day, you know that. Now, please, leave.'

'Alright, Connie, I'm going.' Bette fastened her coat as she found herself ushered out into the rain. 'Give my regards to Roland,' she said but hadn't completed the sentence before the door was slammed behind her.

On the pavement Bette stood for a moment. She was convinced she could make out Connie behind the net curtains standing just far enough back in the room to see out without being seen.

'Have it your own way,' Bette muttered and walked down the street back towards the station, deep in thought.

Connie had slipped up and then lied. She was sure.

But why?

And what had Bette ever done to Dag? Connie clearly thought she had done something, but what?

This was mystery piled on mystery.

So now what? Where else could she turn? Not Roland, he'd do what Connie told him. She'd have to try a different route.

BETTE - KENT, MARCH 1951

Bette waited as the operator connected her call. A soft click sounded at the other end.

'You're through now, caller.'

'Hello, the Grieve residence—who's speaking?'

A woman's voice: clipped, distinguished.

Bette's throat tightened. 'Good morning. May I speak to General Grieve, please?'

'The General is at his club.'

'Oh—I see. Do you know when he'll be back?'

'No, I do not. Who is this?'

The tone was chilly, almost disdainful. Bette pieced things together. 'Ah, is this Mrs Grieve?'

'Does it matter? For your information, my title is Lady Grieve.'

Of course. The General had been knighted. Bette mentally chastised herself; with people like these, titles were everything.

'My apologies, Lady Grieve. I should have introduced myself. My name is Squadron-Leader Baxter and—'

'Good heavens is that what the RAF is coming to?' the woman interrupted.

Bette blinked. 'I'm sorry?'

'Allowing women to become senior officers. That would never have happened in the army.'

The shock prickled along Bette's spine. 'Well, yes, but —'

'In any case, I don't see why you wish to speak to the General. He is retired, and frankly, he was army—not air force.'

'Yes, but this is a personal matter—'

'Ah, so it's personal. In that case, I certainly cannot pass on any message to my husband.'

'But—'

'Good day to you.'

A sharp click ended the call. Bette stared at the receiver for a long moment.

'Caller? The other party has disconnected. Would you like to make another call?' The operator had to repeat herself before Bette replied.

'No. Not just now. Thank you.'

She set the handset back in its cradle, her mind spinning. Douglas had rarely spoken of his father, and he'd always gone by Atkinson-Grieve rather than simply Grieve. Atkinson was his mother's maiden name; Bette was fairly sure Lady Grieve wasn't his mother. She recalled photographs of them at the Festival of Remembrance: Lady Grieve, strikingly unlike Dag, and her first name was Elizabeth, not Margaret, as Dag had once mentioned.

It came together—the likelihood of an affair, the General's son born out of wedlock. That explained Lady Grieve's abruptness, especially at the mention of a 'personal matter.'

Bette exhaled, resolved. She would need a different approach.

And she would try again.

***

Bette waited as the operator attempted to connect her. The sense of déjà vu was almost tangible, but this time she was better prepared and calling later in the day, hopeful that the General might actually be at home. At last, there was a click on the line.

'You're through now, caller.'

'Hello, the Grieve residence?'

Bette's heart sank; the voice was unmistakable.

'Hello, Lady Grieve, it's Bette Baxter. We spoke a few days ago.'

She could feel the temperature drop instantly, as if the chill had bled straight through the wire. She half expected to find frost on the receiver.

'It's you again, is it? I told you I can't—'

'The personal matter I mentioned isn't about the General, if that's your concern. I've never met him. It's about his son.'

A pause—brief, loaded with unspoken emotion.

'Patrick? He's serving in Malaya. I hardly think there's an issue with him.'

'No, not Patrick. His other son—Douglas.'

Now the silence on the line stretched, taut and dangerous.

'Hello? Lady Grieve, are you there?'

'Yes.' Her reply was clipped, harsh enough to sting.

'Thank you. About Douglas—I knew him during the war and—'

'I do not wish to talk about that man.'

Bette gathered herself, forging ahead. 'I understand it must be difficult. Maybe your husband might be willing—?'

'The General won't either. That boy was trouble from the beginning—it carried on into adulthood. He's rotten to the core.'

'Carried on? But Dag is—'

'I told you, we have nothing to say. Do not call again or I will not hesitate to call the police. Good day to you.'

The line went dead.

Bette held the receiver for a few moments before placing it gently back in its cradle. Typical, she thought. Dag had always provoked strong reactions—prickly, difficult, forever at odds with the world. That rift with his family explained a great deal.

Yet, she knew the type: the Grieves, with their rigid codes and cool superiority, always managed civility even when drawing boundaries. Even Lady Grieve, in her icy way, had wished her 'good day' while threatening her with the authorities. Politeness was part of the fabric, the inheritance of their class.

There was another code, too: whatever a man's failings—cad, embezzler, womanizer—if he shared your blood, especially if he died, you never spoke ill of him to outsiders. That was sacred.

But Lady Grieve hadn't used the past tense. If Dag was dead, she'd just shattered a code older than herself.

Unless—he wasn't dead at all. Unless she and the

General both knew it.

It was all circumstantial, yes, but now the evidence was too compelling to ignore.

Leave was coming due. Bette resolved to use it, not for rest, but to chase down the answers she desperately needed.

'That's all right, I don't need to know.' She didn't need to know because she could guess. A certain former navigator and his wife seemed the most likely. 'So, what was the outcome?'

Fiona shrugged. 'The inquiry was inconclusive. The file was closed.'

Inconclusive. Not rejected.

'And yet a second investigation was opened in 1948?'

'Yes.'

'So, what was that about? Why was the case reopened?'

'I can't tell you.'

'Scott, I told you, you won't get into—'

'I know ma-am, it's not that. The whole report has been removed. There is just an entry recording it took place and concluded but the papers themselves were removed and taken away for separate filing. The removal note said that the matter was top secret and that the file where it was now held was closed for fifty years.'

Bette just stared at Fiona in shock. Even she hadn't expected that.

She puffed out her cheeks. This was getting crazy. Was Bette going crazy, hallucinating, inventing all this? No, she was here, the corporal in front of her was real.

'Thank, you, Scott.'

'Will that be all, ma-am?

'Yes — no, wait. Can you look up one more personnel file for me? It might take a while to find so I'll give you, my number.'

Bette took a pen and a piece of paper off the young clerk. She scribbled down her phone number.

One man had the key to all this. If he survived the war and if she could find him, then he'd have answer as to if Dag was alive.

If, if, if. There were too many ifs. She wanted at least one established fact.

LINCOLNSHIRE, MARCH 1951

Bette eased her car up to the gate, waiting for the barrier to rise. The RAF base, her home for the past three years, was draped in its familiar cloak of order: clipped lawns, rigid buildings, the predictable rhythm of uniforms. Yet today, all that steadiness felt oppressive, as if the very bricks were complicit in some unspoken deception. She nodded at the guard, anticipating a casual salute and swift passage, but his formality startled her; he stepped forward, visibly hesitant. Bette rolled down her window.

'Good afternoon, Phillips. Is there a problem?'

'Sorry to trouble you, Ma'am, but the CO asked me to stop you if I saw you. He wants a word.'

She frowned. 'I'm on leave, Phillips. Surely, he knows?'

'He does, Ma'am. But he was very insistent.'

Bette exhaled, resigned. She'd only planned to collect a few clothes before seeing Connie again. Was she being summoned back from leave? Some new emergency? No rumours had reached her ears. Was the RAF heading deeper into Korea? Sending the Lincolns would be madness—everyone knew those aircraft were relics.

'All right, Phillips. I'll go directly. Promise.'

He smiled, relieved, and raised the barrier.

Instead of heading to her quarters, Bette steered

towards the administrative block. The Wing Commander's silhouette loomed in his office window, casting an even longer shadow over her mood. Inside, the outer office buzzed with anticipation.

'You can go straight in, Squadron-Leader.'

She nodded, entered, and rapped on the Wing Commander's door before stepping through.

'Baxter. What have you been up to?'

'Sir?'

He fixed her with a hard stare. 'Bomber Command's been hounding me about you.'

'They have, sir? Why on earth have they done that?'

'Don't feign ignorance, Baxter. You know perfectly well. Bothering families, pestering bereaved parents, intruding on a retired Air-Commodore, and—most notably—your unauthorised visit to the records office today.'

Her jaw dropped. 'Sir, I was only trying to—'

'You were trying to stir up ghosts, Baxter. Chasing a scandal that's best left buried.' He shook his head; disappointment etched in every line. 'I'm surprised by this. You're one of my finest officers.'

'May I speak freely, sir?'

'Of course.'

'I have solid reason to believe a mistake was made in 1944. That a man thought lost—'

'Flight-Sergeant Atkinson-Grieve?'

'Yes, sir.'

'Why does he concern you, Baxter? You're not related, are you?'

'No, sir. It's personal. Strictly private.'

'Ah. I see. It's like that, is it?' The Wing Commander's gaze softened a fraction. 'He's dead, Baxter. I checked myself. They investigated thoroughly.'

'But sir—'

'No more, Baxter.' He held her eyes for a long moment. 'You've built an outstanding career: intelligent, diligent, exceptional—a credit to the service, with every prospect of rising further.'

'Thank you, sir.'

'But you'll jeopardise it chasing phantoms. No more wild goose chases. Is that clear?'

Bette saluted sharply. 'Crystal clear, sir.'

***

The next morning dawned as usual, but Bette lingered in bed after her alarm sounded, resisting the pull of routine. This was unlike her; discipline had always been her trademark.

Yet, with Dag, all that resolve seemed to falter. She ought to move on—let go of the past, let go of him. Was she truly so weak, so vulnerable, left haunted by a man she'd barely known for a handful of weeks, and who had since vanished from her life for seven long years? He'd been a distraction then, and he remained one now.

With determined precision, she forced herself upright. Enough. She would make something of her leave, pay her parents a visit. They always appreciated her presence, even if she rarely enjoyed the encounters. As their only child, it was her duty.

And Bette Baxter always performed her duty.

But as she sank into the bath, her mind wandered back to Dag—and to Connie's sharp words, heavy with accusation and implication. Had she betrayed him? How? What exactly was she supposed to have done? Injustice always struck a nerve with Bette, and she was in no mood to surrender easily.

So, Dag returned, unbidden, to her thoughts. John Hinton had said Dag took part in the airlift. A persistent memory tugged at her: a flight lieutenant at RAF Bramcote—Transport Command's training base—who had joined the staff after the airlift. Bette had led a module for these new officers, and one in particular stood out: an aspiring writer set on chronicling the airlift, amassing notes and photographs for a manuscript.

There was only one problem—his name eluded her. It hovered in her mind, something like Artist, but she knew that wasn't quite right.

Perhaps, by the time she reached Warwickshire, the

MARCH 1951
RAF CRANWELL

Bette found herself waiting again.

It seemed that waiting had become the motif of her recent days: first at Roland and Connie's house, then to talk to General Grieve (a fruitless mission), followed by a round of phone calls to Dag's uncle, the retired Air-Commodore—each conversation more evasive than the last, as if she was being shunted from one polite dead end to another. And now she waited here, at the RAF records office.

She should have come here first. It was, after all, the logical step. Records did not prevaricate or hide behind manners.

But logic was not the guiding star where Dag was concerned. Or perhaps, more truthfully, where she and Dag were concerned. Even the most sensible, grounded person, she reflected, could be thrown into chaos by one pivotal event—or by one individual. For her, Dag was both: the person and the catalyst who had upended her life, sending her down a path lined with uncertainty and longing.

Perhaps, she admitted, she'd been better off before he arrived; before Dag, she'd carved out a niche in service she would never have found in civilian life. After Dag's departure, she'd poured herself into her career, ascending to Squadron-Leader and nurturing a growing reputation as an expert in her field, with a staff under her command.

Renowned, yes—but respected? She was a woman in a man's world. That fact had been made clear in the lecture hall and in countless subtle ways.

And, for all her achievements, she was alone. Despite

her colleagues and subordinates, she remained solitary, insulated by a hard shell she had built herself. She'd learned to keep everyone at arm's length. No one would get close again.

Not after Dag.

She had waited for him for seven years—seven long years—hoping for news she knew would never come.

And yet, the faintest suggestion that he might still be alive was all it took to send her spiralling back to the old pattern, acting now with the reckless energy of a lovesick girl, though she had never indulged in such hopes in her youth.

'Squadron-Leader Baxter?'

The file-clerk's voice broke her reverie.

'Yes?'

She looked up. They were in a side office, painted in the familiar, institutional shade of RAF green. The clerk had led her here and brought her a cup of strong, copper-coloured tea, mercifully robust.

'I've found the Flight-Sergeant's file, ma'am,' the clerk said. 'He is, indeed, recorded as confirmed dead after a mission to France on the night of the 4th to 5th of June 1944.'

The girl could not have been more than nineteen—hardly more than a child—but bright, with an earnestness betrayed by the way she bit her lower lip, as if there was more she wished to say but could not.

'Thank you,' Bette replied. 'Is there anything else in the file?'

The clerk glanced nervously toward the open door.

'I don't know if I should...'

'Come in and close the door,' Bette said gently, offering an encouraging smile. The clerk obeyed. 'What's your name, Corporal?'

'Scott, ma'am. Fiona Scott.'

'Fiona, that's a lovely name. Now, Scott, you won't get in any trouble for this. Tell me—what did you find?'

Fiona puffed out her cheeks, mustering her courage.

'Well, ma'am, his file is peculiar. Very peculiar. I've never seen anything quite like it.'

Bette nodded, unsurprised. 'I expected as much. I was involved in some of the Flight-Sergeant's operations in 1944, so that doesn't startle me. Tell me, what makes it so odd?'

Fiona looked relieved. 'Well, for one thing, it was a lot thicker than I expected. That was why I...'

Her voice trailed off.

Bette smiled. 'It's all right, you were curious. That's fine. Just tell me what you saw.'

Fiona frowned. 'But we're told not to—'

'I told you; you're not in trouble. I'm just looking for confirmation of what we already know.'

Bette was in uniform even though she was on leave and this lie somehow made her starched shirt collar rub against the skin of her neck as if in punishment.

'All right,' said Fiona. 'I did take a quick look. Sergeant Atkinson-Grieve did nearly a full tour on Halifaxes in 1943 to 44. This was after quite a checkered time during training when he got into quite a few scrapes and this carried on into his service life. He was confined to barracks a couple of times and his commanding officer recorded that he had an issue with authority.'

Bette couldn't help but smile. 'That sounds like Dag,' she murmured. Fiona looked at her, puzzlement on her face. 'I'm sorry, carry on, Scott.'

'Yes, ma-am. Well, that's where the file got odd. It seemed like the records for several months had been removed. There was a partial record for the aftermath of the Sergeant's 29th mission. Something dreadful had happened during it, and his crew had refused to fly with him again. Sergeant Atkinson-Grieve was withdrawn from flying for psychological assessment. After that there is a total blank for several months. That shouldn't happen, there should have been some entries, even if he was posted away or was receiving treatment somewhere but there was nothing. There were signs though, some torn paper, that suggested there had been something there, but it had been ripped out.' Fiona looked troubled, almost as if she was the one responsible for the file's desecration.

'Go on,' said Bette. 'Where does the file pick up?'

'He was posted in May to a special duties flight near Grantham.'

'That would be 1590 flight.'

'Yes, ma-am.'

Bette bit her lip. She remembered that night, the night Dag went down, being called into Ambrose's office, his demanding that she tell him the truth about Dag's past, that she should tell him the truth because, if she did, Dag's aircraft would be recalled.

All she had to do was tell Ambrose that Dag had been found LMF, the fact that Dag's uncle had manipulated the record so this career-ending fact was suppressed and that would be it, the man she loved would be saved — saved by being condemned.

An impossible position.

She realised Fiona was still speaking.

'Sorry, Scott, what did you say?'

'I was saying that this was where the Sergeant's service record ends. His aircraft was reported missing on the night of 4th /5th June as I said. The loss of the aircraft and all but one of the crew was confirmed when the one survivor reached Southampton on June 9th having been repatriated by the American forces on Omaha beach via a returning LST.'

Bette's eyes widened. 'A survivor? Of Dag's — I mean, Flight-Sergeant Atkinson-Grieve's crew?'

'Yes, Ma-am. The navigator.'

'Flight/Sergeant Khan?'

'Yes ma-am.'

Bette shook her head. There was a survivor. Faz had survived, she hadn't known that. Why hadn't anyone told her?

Bette saw Fiona swallow. Did that mean there was more in the file? Time to be bold, to keep the young woman talking.

'So, about the follow up?' Bette could see that she'd not said something that surprised Fiona: she'd guessed right. 'The file on Sergeant Atkinson-Grieve didn't end there, did it?'

Fiona nodded. 'No, it didn't. There was a supplement, two in fact, that covered investigations carried out in 1945 and 1948.'

Investigations? What investigations? Bette thought quickly. It could only be one thing. 'Into whether the information about whether Sergeant Atkinson-Grieve was dead was correct?'

'Yes, ma-am.'

'Why were they done? And what did they find?'

Fiona frowned. 'The first was instigated by a friend, a former service colleague of the sergeant.'

Bette raised her eyebrows. That was interesting.

'Who raised the question?'

Fiona shook her head. 'I really shouldn't...'

'That's all right, I don't need to know.' She didn't need to know because she could guess. A certain former navigator and his wife seemed the most likely. 'So, what was the outcome?'

Fiona shrugged. 'The inquiry was inconclusive. The file was closed.'

Inconclusive. Not rejected.

'And yet a second investigation was opened in 1948?'

'Yes.'

'So, what was that about? Why was the case reopened?'

'I can't tell you.'

'Scott, I told you, you won't get into—'

'I know ma-am, it's not that. The whole report has been removed. There is just an entry recording it took place and concluded but the papers themselves were removed and taken away for separate filing. The removal note said that the matter was top secret and that the file where it was now held was closed for fifty years.'

Bette just stared at Fiona in shock. Even she hadn't expected that.

She puffed out her cheeks. This was getting crazy. Was Bette going crazy, hallucinating, inventing all this? No, she was here, the corporal in front of her was real.

'Thank, you, Scott.'

'Will that be all, ma-am?

'Yes — no, wait. Can you look up one more personnel file for me? It might take a while to find so I'll give you, my number.'

Bette took a pen and a piece of paper off the young clerk. She scribbled down her phone number.

One man had the key to all this. If he survived the war and if she could find him, then he'd have answer as to if Dag was alive.

If, if, if. There were too many ifs. She wanted at least one established fact.

LINCOLNSHIRE, MARCH 1951

Bette eased her car up to the gate, waiting for the barrier to rise. The RAF base, her home for the past three years, was draped in its familiar cloak of order: clipped lawns, rigid buildings, the predictable rhythm of uniforms. Yet today, all that steadiness felt oppressive, as if the very bricks were complicit in some unspoken deception. She nodded at the guard, anticipating a casual salute and swift passage, but his formality startled her; he stepped forward, visibly hesitant. Bette rolled down her window.

'Good afternoon, Phillips. Is there a problem?'

'Sorry to trouble you, Ma'am, but the CO asked me to stop you if I saw you. He wants a word.'

She frowned. 'I'm on leave, Phillips. Surely, he knows?'

'He does, Ma'am. But he was very insistent.'

Bette exhaled, resigned. She'd only planned to collect a few clothes before seeing Connie again. Was she being summoned back from leave? Some new emergency? No rumours had reached her ears. Was the RAF heading deeper into Korea? Sending the Lincolns would be madness—everyone knew those aircraft were relics.

'All right, Phillips. I'll go directly. Promise.'

He smiled, relieved, and raised the barrier.

Instead of heading to her quarters, Bette steered

towards the administrative block. The Wing Commander's silhouette loomed in his office window, casting an even longer shadow over her mood. Inside, the outer office buzzed with anticipation.

'You can go straight in, Squadron-Leader.'

She nodded, entered, and rapped on the Wing Commander's door before stepping through.

'Baxter. What have you been up to?'

'Sir?'

He fixed her with a hard stare. 'Bomber Command's been hounding me about you.'

'They have, sir? Why on earth have they done that?'

'Don't feign ignorance, Baxter. You know perfectly well. Bothering families, pestering bereaved parents, intruding on a retired Air-Commodore, and—most notably—your unauthorised visit to the records office today.'

Her jaw dropped. 'Sir, I was only trying to—'

'You were trying to stir up ghosts, Baxter. Chasing a scandal that's best left buried.' He shook his head; disappointment etched in every line. 'I'm surprised by this. You're one of my finest officers.'

'May I speak freely, sir?'

'Of course.'

'I have solid reason to believe a mistake was made in 1944. That a man thought lost—'

'Flight-Sergeant Atkinson-Grieve?'

'Yes, sir.'

'Why does he concern you, Baxter? You're not related, are you?'

'No, sir. It's personal. Strictly private.'

'Ah. I see. It's like that, is it?' The Wing Commander's gaze softened a fraction. 'He's dead, Baxter. I checked myself. They investigated thoroughly.'

'But sir—'

'No more, Baxter.' He held her eyes for a long moment. 'You've built an outstanding career: intelligent, diligent, exceptional—a credit to the service, with every prospect of rising further.'

'Thank you, sir.'

'But you'll jeopardise it chasing phantoms. No more wild goose chases. Is that clear?'

Bette saluted sharply. 'Crystal clear, sir.'

***

The next morning dawned as usual, but Bette lingered in bed after her alarm sounded, resisting the pull of routine. This was unlike her; discipline had always been her trademark.

Yet, with Dag, all that resolve seemed to falter. She ought to move on—let go of the past, let go of him. Was she truly so weak, so vulnerable, left haunted by a man she'd barely known for a handful of weeks, and who had since vanished from her life for seven long years? He'd been a distraction then, and he remained one now.

With determined precision, she forced herself upright. Enough. She would make something of her leave, pay her parents a visit. They always appreciated her presence, even if she rarely enjoyed the encounters. As their only child, it was her duty.

And Bette Baxter always performed her duty.

But as she sank into the bath, her mind wandered back to Dag—and to Connie's sharp words, heavy with accusation and implication. Had she betrayed him? How? What exactly was she supposed to have done? Injustice always struck a nerve with Bette, and she was in no mood to surrender easily.

So, Dag returned, unbidden, to her thoughts. John Hinton had said Dag took part in the airlift. A persistent memory tugged at her: a flight lieutenant at RAF Bramcote— Transport Command's training base—who had joined the staff after the airlift. Bette had led a module for these new officers, and one in particular stood out: an aspiring writer set on chronicling the airlift, amassing notes and photographs for a manuscript.

There was only one problem—his name eluded her. It hovered in her mind, something like Artist, but she knew that wasn't quite right.

Perhaps, by the time she reached Warwickshire, the

name would return.

***

'Hello, Squadron-Leader. This is quite the surprise.'

Bette thought so too, though at least she knew his name now. It was there, clear as day, on his office door.

'Ah, well, Flight-Lieutenant Painter—I happened to be passing, and I remembered your airlift project. I wondered how your research was progressing?'

Painter looked startled, and for a fleeting moment, somewhat wary. Did he suspect a senior officer's ulterior motive? Bette, weary of subterfuge after so many recent deceits, decided to drop the act.

She drew a measured breath. 'All right, Painter, I admit I have a personal reason for asking.' His alarm seemed to deepen, and she couldn't help but smile. 'Not that sort of reason. I'm interested in your book—or rather, the photographs you've gathered.'

She outlined her purpose.

'This is unofficial, of course—entirely personal. If you'd prefer not to help, I'd understand.'

Painter shook his head. 'I'd be delighted, Squadron-Leader. I love discussing the airlift and the book. Over the past couple of years, I've collected hundreds of prints. Most of them won't make it into the final draft, but I'd be glad to share them. Shall we begin?'

'Yes, please. Lead the way.'

***

Three hours later, Bette was back in her car.

She placed the foolscap envelope on the seat next to her, all thoughts about heading to Manchester and her parents gone. She knew where she had to go instead. But she needed to wait until she had the address.

She turned the car back in the direction of her squadron.

She'd have to wait for Fiona Scott to come through with the information she now needed more than ever.

LEICESTER, MARCH 1951

Bette sat in the waiting room, surrounded by the muffled chorus of coughs and restless shuffles. Even in the haze of noise and movement, she was lost in her thoughts. Nearby, a young mother attempted to soothe a wailing baby, exhaustion etched under her eyes. Two little boys wove through the maze of chairs, giggling as they darted behind patients, while their mothers—deep in conversation—barely glanced up at the chaos unfolding at their feet. The older clientele watched with a mixture of exasperation and resignation.

The receptionist, her patience clearly fraying, tried one last time to deter Bette. 'Are you sure you want to wait? It could be hours, you know.'

'I'll wait,' Bette replied, her voice resolute.

The receptionist sighed. 'Well, suit yourself,' she muttered, turning back to her paperwork.

Bette picked up a battered copy of The Illustrated London News, flicking through the faded pages without interest. She'd waited nearly seven years already—what were a few more hours? The envelope she'd brought weighed heavily on her lap, its contents pressing on her mind as much as the paper pressed against her skirt.

***

Finally, the door to the doctor's office opened. An elderly woman, hunched and leaning on her stick, shuffled out, pausing only to thank the doctor.

'Try to eat plenty of fresh fruit, Mrs Bailey, lots of vitamin C,' the doctor said in a kindly but distracted tone.

'My son's a good boy, but that wife of his...' the old woman began, but the doctor's attention was elsewhere. He'd spotted Bette.

'I'm sorry, Dr Khan,' the receptionist said. 'This lady insisted on waiting.'

'That's all right. I know her. Bette, please—come in.' He stood aside, gesturing for her to enter.

'Thank you, Faz,' she said, stepping past him into his office.

***

'So, is he mistaken? Or is Squadron Leader Hinton seeing ghosts?' Bette, once the door closed behind her, had immediately recounted what John Hinton had told her.

Faz ran a hand through his hair. 'I don't know the man, but he must be. I was there. I know what happened.'

'Which was?' she pressed.

He exhaled, frustration creasing his brow. 'It's all in the report. Do I have to recount it again?'

'Humour me,' she said gently.

He nodded, resigned. 'All right. Our aircraft was shot down over Normandy. Dag stayed with the plane and survived the crash. I managed to bail out, but we were both captured. We escaped but were picked up again. The resistance freed us, and we made it to the coast. In a firefight, I was wounded. Dag was killed.'

Bette absorbed this quietly. 'You were left behind and rescued by advancing troops.'

'Yes.'

'So close to surviving,' she murmured.

Faz's voice was softer now. 'He was, yes.'

'You saw his body? Identified him?' she asked.

Faz hesitated. 'Yes, I did. But it was later recovered, so the authorities had his dog tags.'

Bette nodded.

'So,' Faz continued with a forced smile, 'whoever Squadron Leader Hinton is, he must be mistaken.'

Bette didn't answer, just watched Faz until his smile faded. He looked nervously at the envelope in her hand.

She considered ending it there but decided to continue. She stood up. 'Thanks, Faz. You're right, the squadron leader must have been confused. Odd, though—he knew Dag

29

well.' She offered her hand. Faz shook it, his palm sweaty.

'Yes, strange things happen with memory. Stress can play tricks.'

'I know,' Bette replied, letting go and walking to a photo of Dag's Halifax crew. At their feet was the cross Dag had described from one of his missions over France, collected in the wing of his machine as the Halifax had swept low over a French church. Almost too low. After a pause, she said, 'You've done well here—a respected doctor.'

Faz smiled. 'My father would've been proud. He'd almost lost hope I'd follow him.'

'You never flew again after Normandy, did you?'

'No.'

'Why not?'

'I was wounded.'

'Just your leg—you left hospital after about a month, right?'

He nodded. 'About that.'

'And you hadn't finished a tour?'

'No, but, Bette, why the interrogation?'

She glanced at photos on his desk, then at the door, considering leaving. But she sat again. 'Tell me the story—the full story.'

'There's nothing more than what's in the report. What are you getting at?'

'I want to hear about Normandy and Dag's last hours. That's all.'

Faz sighed, checking the time. 'Honestly, I wanted to get home early tonight. I don't see the point in revisiting this.'

'I know, but I need to hear it—from you—in detail.'

'Why bring up painful memories? Dag is dead.'

'I know. I've read the files, but I need to understand— for closure.' She placed a hand on his. 'Please, Faz.'

He nodded. 'Alright. Where should I start?'

'That first night in Normandy.'

Faz stared at his desk for a moment, then began.

0121 HOURS
5TH JUNE 1944

This couldn't be real. This had to be a movie.

It was as vivid as if he was watching a film; except this reel wasn't in black and white like in the cinema, this was in vivid colour made more so by being played out in the dark of night.

But he knew it was real. The flak. The cannon shells, yellow parabolas in the sky, arching up then flashing by. The hits tearing through the thin aluminium, shattering the Perspex of the bomb aimer's position, the blood fountaining from the radio operator, decapitated and turned to a grotesque twitching puppet, the man's blood that had stained Faz's uniform visibly scarlet thanks to the blaze from the burning engine and the sheets of flame from the wing tanks.

Faz shook himself out of his stupor.

He knew the Halifax was doomed and that Dag was doing the only thing left to him: trying to climb to give his crew a chance to bail out. But the bailout alarm hadn't been set off. Faz opened the hatch but then waited: They weren't supposed to go until ordered or until the alarm rang. His senses screamed at him to go; his training made him stay.

He was almost too late, the final lurch down as C-Charlie entered its death dive was so violent it threw him up and pinned him to the roof of his position in the nose. Then, suddenly, somehow, he was outside the burning aircraft, tumbling through the night alongside it, desperately searching for the D-ring of his parachute, unable to find it, almost giving up but then snagging something and pulling just in case. Moments later three things happened virtually simultaneously; an almighty jerk as his chute opened; the Halifax appeared to shoot forward as if it were suddenly accelerating; and, finally, he hit the ground, the force driving the breath from his body.

He was stunned, his brain scrambled, gulping air but his lungs still in spasm, empty, aware that he was still moving, bouncing off the grass, being dragged through foliage, twigs, branches and thorns tearing at him. Abruptly his mind cleared enough to realise he was being dragged by his chute, but it took a long few seconds to find the quick release, and a few moments longer to tumble off the last of his momentum. When he had stopped, he rolled over on his back and just lay in the rich Norman grass, panting.

How long he stayed there he wasn't sure but, at last, he forced himself to his feet. He was vaguely aware that there was something wrong with his knee, but he was able to dismiss it. He could see the remains of C-Charlie burning a few hundred yards away. He started to limp towards the wreck but then torches and shouts showed a patrol was closing in. Perhaps he would have continued if it wasn't for his wife and his unborn first.

He wanted to see them, desperately. He couldn't be caught, he just couldn't. Before he knew it, he'd turned and ran.

The guilt started when he stopped running and settled down into a limping walk. His leg was now on fire, stiffening up all the time. He needed to find somewhere to hide, to rest and recover.

But still he'd thought about what he'd done, how he'd left them.

It was hopeless, he'd told himself, the flames had spread so fast that anyone inside, Dag, Doddy, Mo, Fritz, the lot of them, even if they'd survived the impact, they'd be gone. He prayed to Allah it was quick for them.

But still the guilt was there.

It wasn't getting any better.

***

'You thought Dag was dead?'

Faz nodded. 'Of course.' He shook his head, 'You must know how hard it was for crews to get out of bombers? Yes, sure it was better in the old Hallibag than in Lancs but for the pilot? At that altitude? Not a chance. Yes, I was sure then that he was dead. That they all were.'

Bette nodded. 'But you were captured anyway?'

'Not until the evening.'

***

1650 HOURS
5TH JUNE 1944

Faz couldn't get comfortable. It wasn't just the pain from his strains and bruises: he was in shock too, he could recognise that. It was shock mixed with disbelief. He was an evader, down in occupied France, being hunted. Why now? All right, he was alive but when would he get to see his baby? Would he or she even be a baby when he finally got home?

He shook his head. He *was* alive. Not like the rest. He should be thankful for that.

He stretched his leg out, massaging the joints which had borne the impact of his hard landing as best he could. A full day and the swelling had now come out. The adrenalin that had flowed through his system that enabled him to run, collect and hide his parachute and get away from the crash site and the burning Halifax had long since gone. Now everything just hurt, his knee was immobile, he could barely hobble.

How could he get away?
How could he get home?

1920 HOURS
5TH JUNE 1944

He had heard the German patrol about thirty minutes before. Now they were getting closer.

He tried to get deeper into the hedge where he was hiding. The voices got closer. Perhaps they'd miss him? But then he heard the dog bark. They were on his scent. It was hopeless.

He scrambled out, hands up.

He thought it would go easier on him if he did that.

As it was, he was grabbed roughly, was pushed and shoved, kicked and then dragged along when he'd fallen and received a nasty bite on his left hand from the patrol's Alsatian which numbed it and stung like the devil.

'Who are you? Was that your aircraft that crashed this morning?' The officer in charge of the patrol spoke good English.

'1838236, Khan, Fight-Sergeant.'

The officer didn't hesitate. He slapped Faz hard in the face.

'Answer me!' he'd yelled. 'Now! Now!'

'1838236, Khan, Fight-Sergeant.'

Faz ducked away from the next blow.

'You will regret that. I suggest you talk.'

'I am a prisoner of war. You should follow the regulations of the Genev—'

This time was not able to avoid the blow.

2250 HOURS
5TH JUNE 1944

Faz found little comfort in being indoors; if anything, the chill of the cellar gripped him more keenly than the cool June night outside. He shivered, uncertain whether it was the lingering cold or the shock of capture that unsettled him most.

Instead of swift interrogation, he had been bundled into the cellar of a farmhouse commandeered by the patrol. The room was damp and shadowed, the air thick with the scent of earth and old stone. Upstairs, he'd glimpsed the farmer, his wife, and their teenage granddaughter—each watching in silence as the German officer, speaking rough French, explained their need for a place to hold a prisoner. That was how Faz found himself behind a locked door, left to the uneasy company of his thoughts and, presumably, a solitary guard above.

News that the patrol had gone searching for other survivors from C-Charlie brought a faint flicker of hope. Perhaps someone else had made it out. Yet, he knew better than to let optimism take root; experience told him such hopes were often dashed just as quickly as they appeared.

As he passed the local family, Faz noticed a brief, wordless exchange—a glance, a nod—between the farmer and his granddaughter. The Maquis were active in Normandy; it was, after all, the reason his unit was here tonight. Perhaps they belonged to the resistance. Perhaps, if fate was kind, they might attempt a rescue. Or was that just another fragile hope, a desperate clutch at possibility?

He found himself wishing for their intervention, even as he wrestled with the consequences—if they tried and failed, their suffering would be added to his already heavy conscience. Was it selfish to want deliverance at such a cost? Perhaps. But the urge to survive, to make it home, burned brighter than any guilt or fear. He just had to get back.

0003 HOURS
6TH JUNE 1944

The rattle of keys outside the cellar door was heralded by guttural voices drifting from the kitchen. Faz was already on his feet when the door swung open, anticipation taut in his chest. Had the patrol found someone else? He swallowed, pulse flickering with a vain hope.

But only a lone guard appeared, his presence dissolving any flicker of optimism.

'Come. You come.'

The German was older, his uniform careworn and threadbare, a far cry from the imposing façade of the Aryan elite. It told Faz everything—he was in the custody of a second-rate, second-line unit, likely tasked with ferrying prisoners while others, accompanied by dogs, swept the countryside. The specifics of his destination—an interrogation cell, perhaps—remained unclear, but the outcome was certain: captivity.

His companions were younger, their faces sharp with sallow disinterest. Eastern Europeans, Faz guessed—Ukrainian or Polish, perhaps. It didn't matter. Their bored, restless glances revealed everything: they would rather be anywhere else.

And, in truth, so would he.

Shepherded through the kitchen, Faz caught the French family seated at their table, expressions carved with silent resentment. He tried to offer them a reassuring smile, a mute acknowledgment that he understood their plight—that coercion, not complicity, had placed them here.

He wished he believed his own reassurance.

One of the guards lingered, eyes on the granddaughter, who met his gaze with glacial hostility. The squad leader barked an order at the man. He blew a kiss at the girl and hustled Faz out.

Outside, a truck idled, its canvas flaps snapping in the brisk wind. Faz glanced upward at clouds tearing across the moonlit sky, the full moon intermittently smothered in grey. Tonight was no night to be flying.

Yet the sky was alive. As the German prodded him towards the truck, Faz caught the distant drone of aero engines above the wind's fret. Leaves shivered, branches moaned, but the rising thrum eclipsed all else.

'Up, up,' urged the German, his voice laced with unease as he hurried Faz along, eyes darting upwards. The engines grew louder, urgent, and relentless—a bomber stream, surely, and flying dangerously low. The target was close.

And Faz, in the thick of it, could only wonder whom fate would favour tonight.

Faz hoped the bomb-aimers did their job well. He didn't fancy being on the receiving end of a stack of thousand-pounders.

'Schnell, schnell. Hoch, hoch.'

The German's urgency was unmistakable, and Faz found himself half-stepping, half-dragged into the truck by the waiting soldiers within. Their anxious faces tilted skyward, listening to the mounting tumult above. Suddenly, the thunder of a flak battery erupted, soon joined by another; the deep booms of the 88s briefly pierced the night before being swallowed by the relentless drone of approaching aircraft.

As they bounced along the track, Faz got glimpses of the sky out of the back of the truck. Flashes from the bursting flak and searchlights lit it up. There was, he judged five to six tenths cloud cover, so it was hard to make out the aircraft. Then the clouds cleared, and a searchlight found one of them. Faz gasped; it was a Dakota, and it wasn't alone; perhaps fifty or more were in the stream.

And black objects were tumbling out of them.

'Fallschirmjäger!' someone yelled.

'Scheisse!'

Someone was muttering, saying the same words over and over.

'Pan jest moim pasterzem, Pan jest moim pasterzem.'

It was the guard opposite, he was rocking back and forwards, alternately casting worried looks out into the night, then staring fixedly at the floor, all the time repeating the same words; 'Pan jest moim pasterzem, Pan jest moim pasterzem.'

Polish, the man was Polish, Faz had met so many in the RAF that he could recognise it and what he was saying; The Lord is my shepherd.

'Halt die Klappe, du verdammter Seelachs,' another guard growled but still the rocking and praying continued.

Abruptly the truck lurched to the left, throwing Faz across the back into the praying guard but only momentarily as it swung violently back the other way, the Pole now pinning Faz against the canvas. The truck tipped, hung for a moment, and then violently tipped over, the cabin a tangle of legs, arms and bodies. It seemed it was certain to roll over and crush them but, at the last moment, it fell back onto its wheels. The engine stopped.

The canvas was distorted, Faz could feel branches sticking into him through the thick material. He and the guards scrambled over each other to get out, Faz actually holding a hand out to pull one of them up through the now twisted opening at the back.

'Danke,' the guard said, then quickly reached for his rifle, pointing it at Faz who put his hands up.

'No, no, I'm not going anywhere. Friend, friend!'

The man seemed to understand and, mollified, lowered his gun. Both he and Faz started as shots rang out. The guard dived to the ground, cocking his rifle, he looked around for their assailant. Faz joined him in the dirt, also looking for where the shots were coming from. He soon found it; somewhere up in the trees to the right of them there were flashes coming from about thirty feet off the ground. The guard loosed off a couple of shots and, abruptly, the reports from the trees stopped. Still, they all remained in the dirt for a few more seconds before cautiously getting to their feet.

Faz surveyed the scene, the pale moonlight painting a surreal tableau around the battered truck, its cab wedged deep into the hedge. Six figures stood scattered in the aftermath—himself among them—each tense and uncertain. Before them, sprawled on the dirt track, lay a parachute-draped silhouette, ghostly and still. Faz suspected it was an errant parachutist whose sudden descent had sent the driver careening off course.

A sharp command cut through the night; a rifle jabbed into Faz's ribs as a soldier began a cautious approach toward the motionless figure lying ahead. Like a wary hunter confronting a wounded beast, the guard first lobbed a handful of stones, testing for any sign of life. When the body remained inert, he crept closer, nudging it with the muzzle of his gun.

'Hey! Aufstehen. Aufstehen!' he barked, voice taut with impatience.

The body didn't stir. Gathering his nerve, the soldier peeled back the parachute.

'Was zum Teufel?' he muttered, astonishment etched across his face.

Faz understood the confusion instantly—the figure beneath the canopy was so diminutive it seemed almost childlike. As the soldier hoisted the dummy, Faz realised it was nothing more than a three-foot-tall mannequin, roughly dressed to mimic a paratrooper. Suddenly, two sharp cracks rang out from within, startling the soldier so completely that he dropped the dummy in fright.

'Firecrackers!' The voice came from Faz's left. 'Brilliant.'

It took a moment for Faz to register that the man had spoken in English, and a fraction more for him to recognise who it was.

'Dag!'

The man stared at him in disbelief for a full second, then threw his arms around Faz.

'Faz! You're alive!'

The two comrades hugged each other as the aerial armada continued to rumble overhead.

0022 HOURS
6TH JUNE 1944

'Oh my God, Faz. I thought you were dead.'

'I was sure you were, Dag.'

They were pulled roughly apart, Faz being shoved bodily away.

'Nein! NEIN! Kein sprechen.'

One of the guards pointed his rifle at both me in turn. Faz held up his hands.

'All right, all right.'

The troops were tense, and, aware that any mistake could be fatal, Faz hoped Dag understood this was not the moment for impulsiveness. A shout came from the crashed truck—one man forced his way into the hedge, struggling to open the cab door and signalling for help.

'Move,' ordered the guard with the rifle, pushing them forward to keep them in view.

'Come on Dag, Faz muttered.'

Dag fell into step alongside him.

They walked beyond the cab. 'Stop, stop. Wait. Wait.'

The guard seemed to know a few words of English. Faz wondered if he understood more. That might be useful. Whatever, he kept a wary eye on them whilst the other three members of the squad tried to force a way through the foliage to get to the far side of the cabin.

'Someone must be trapped,' Dag whispered.

'Kein sprechen! Kein sprechen!'

The guard jabbed his rifle at Dag who grunted in pain.

Faz could see the rescuers were struggling to clear the branches of the hedge around where the cab had come to rest. A flash from the air — probably a flak burst — revealed there was someone there, Faz could see a bloodied arm. The driver? Possibly, but there was no sign of the older German squad leader. Perhaps both of them had been thrown through the truck's windscreen as it swerved and rolled.

'Shit, they've been crushed,' muttered Dag.

'Kein sprechen! Ruhig, oder ich schieße.'

'Nicht schieße,' said Faz. 'Look, I might be able to help. I've got some medical training.'

The guard frowned. He looked blankly at him.

Faz pointed at himself. 'Medic. Doctor...well, nearly.'

'Doktor?'

'Ja, ja.'

'You come.' He beckoned Faz towards the cab, perhaps forgetting about Dag, but the latter did, at least, follow rather than run as Faz limped painfully on his stiff knee. He forced his way through the foliage to get to the front of the truck. The other guards already there looked surprised.

'Doktor, doktor,' explained their captor.

The guards seemed to understand; one reached down to pull Faz up the last part to where they had cleared some of the foliage. The other shone his torch so Faz could see. He knelt down as best he could with his immobile knee to get a better look.

Now he could see that both driver and the squad leader had, indeed, been thrown half through the screen as the truck crashed; the weight of the bulky older man probably having carried him further than the younger, lighter man. They were together, both pinned by the truck's cab, the driver trapped by his torso, the squad leader twisted and smashed into the sturdy trunk of a tree. Faz felt for a pulse for the squad leader; there was none.

'He's dead,' he said. 'Tot, kaput.'

One of the guards crossed himself.

He did the same for the driver. This time it was different, there was a pulse, though the man's heart was racing.

'This man is alive,' he said. He tried to assess the extent

of the man's injuries. The one thing he could tell was that his arm was broken, it was likely his ribs were too, given where he was pinned. He had to have spinal injuries too, but the greatest risk was going to be from shock and from his ribs puncturing a lung. Was the man's skin blue? That would show a lack of oxygen. He couldn't see the man's face but could the nape of his neck; yes, that did hint at a blueness. But was that from damage to his lungs or simply from being pinned?

Whatever, there was only one course to take.

'We've got to push the truck back off him,' he said.

The guards looked blankly at him.

'Push, push!' Faz used his hands to mime what he wanted.

'Ja,' said one.

'Es ist zu schwer,' said another. 'Too…groß.'

'Groß. Heavy?'

'Ja, ja.'

'We must try though.'

Faz got painfully to his feet and scrambled back down to the track. He started tugging at the frame of the truck, trying to use his weight to pull it back. Moments later he was joined by Dag and the other guards.

Faz knew straight away it was hopeless; if there had been twenty or so of them, they might have had a chance; five was not enough.

'We need a lever. A fulcrum.'

The guards looked blankly at him. He searched his memory for the few words of Polish he'd picked up from the Poles he'd served with. Mostly though those words had been about girls and partying, as well as some choice swearwords.

'Punkt podparcia. Dewignia,' he tried.

'Dźwignia?' one of the men replied.

'Yes, Dźwignia. Lever.' Faz mimed pulling on a long pole.

The guards exchanged looks. One nodded and started looking around.

But before he could go and look a yell of terror came from Dag

'Bloody hell, look out!'

Looking back over his shoulder, Faz froze, staring in

45

horror.

A Dakota, ablaze from wingtip to wingtip, both propellers stopped, less than a hundred feet up was heading straight for them.

LEICESTER
MARCH 1951

'That would have been one of the first wave of paratroops,' said Bette

Faz shrugged. 'Would it? Well, if it was it wasn't a great start to the invasion. Those poor bastards in those Dakotas. No armour, no self-sealing tanks, no guns and coming in low and slow. They were sitting ducks. Damned heroes, the poor sods who had to fly those things.'

'I'm not sure I'd have felt like that at that moment.' Bette allowed herself a smile.

Faz just nodded his agreement.

0031 HOURS
JUNE 6TH 1944

Faz was forcefully pulled from the hedge onto the track. He was reminded of his youth, of the hated school rugby matches, when he would be tackled by significantly larger opponents—especially when he hit the ground and was pushed into the dirt by another's weight pressing down on him.

However, the similarities ended there. Unlike rugby, here there was screaming, a powerful rush of air, a surge of heat, a strong stink of petrol, a loud crash, and the sound of metal colliding with something solid.

Convinced he had died and was in Hell, Faz then experienced a stark transition; the overwhelming heat vanished abruptly and was replaced by complete darkness, as though he had been immersed in freezing water.

The weight lifted off him and he was able to move. He sat up.

He was on the track alongside Dag in the dirt along with two of the guards. He looked for the truck that they had been straining to move. It wasn't next to them anymore. It was upside down, wheels pointing to the sky, on top of the hedge and was silhouetted in red by the fire burning in the field beyond.

That would be the Dakota.

Or what was left of it after hitting the truck.

'Jan, Jan, wo ist Jan?'

One of the guards was on his feet. He ran towards the truck. The other shouted something which Faz didn't catch but made his intentions clear by pointing his gun at Faz and Dag.

'We're not going anywhere, mate,' said Dag. Faz saw him look towards the truck. 'Jesus,' he muttered. 'Oh God.'

Faz looked as well and wished that he hadn't. A vision from a nightmare had appeared at the top of the slope, a man, certainly, but one who was ablaze, the fire completely enveloping him. He made no sound, he didn't scream, nor did he run, he just picked his way over the hedge as if he was out on a country ramble.

'Jan, Jan!'

The man turned, raised his hand in greeting, then collapsed, rolling into the roadside ditch, the flames hissing and spitting as they hit the water and a cloud of steam enveloping the body. The light dimmed as the flames went out.

'Jan, nein.' The guard plunged into the ditch, pulling the man's body from the water. 'Jan, nie.' He turned to look at Faz 'Ty, ty jesteś lekarzem, pomóż mu,' he shouted.

Faz frowned. 'What? What are you saying?'

'Doktor, doktor!' the man pleaded.

Faz looked at the other guard who nodded and urged Faz to go over with a wave of the barrel of his rifle.

Once there Faz wished he 'd stayed where he was. The stench was dreadful; the stink of petrol mingled with smoke and the sickly-sweet stench of burnt flesh. The man's uniform had been incinerated, it was impossible to tell where cloth stopped, and skin began. There was an exception, the man's hands. Here the skin hung off like wax off a candle. The gleam of white showed where he'd been burnt down to the bone.

But he was alive. Somehow, he was still alive.

'You're going to be all right, chap,' said Faz. He looked up at the guard who held his friend. 'Morphine, have you got Morphine with you?'

'Morfina? Nie, nie mamy żadnego.'

'Hell,' Faz said. He looked down at the man. The shock had protected him but what would it be like when that wore off? It was unthinkable.

'Poprawi się?' Faz frowned. 'He will better?' The man repeated in broken English.

Faz shook his head. The guard nodded. 'Iść,' he

murmured. 'Go,' he said more firmly. He reached for his rifle which lay at his side.

Faz got to his feet and moved away. He turned his back, listening to the low murmur as the man talked gently to his injured companion.

The gunshot was remarkably quiet, drowned out by the crackle of fire from the truck which was now firmly ablaze.

Faz and Dag stood by the other guard. Faz realised that none of them could bear to look over at where the burned man and his companion lay.

Above them the drone of the aircraft continued.

0056 HOURS
6TH JUNE 1944

Faz and Dag sat on the cool grass by the hedgerow, across from the twisted wreckage of the truck. Their wrists, chafed and bound with strips of canvas sliced from the tarpaulin, ached with each small movement. Nearby, the two guards, deep in a heated discussion, had withdrawn a few paces, their voices carrying just above the dying crackle of the burning Dakota. Overhead, the night sky blazed with the constant, distant illumination of flares—artificial dawn on the eve of chaos.

Of the patrol leader and the driver, pinned when the truck overturned, there was no sign.

'I can't believe you're alive, Faz,' Dag said. 'I thought I'd killed you.'

Faz frowned. 'Dag, why would you think that? You stayed with the bus and gave me time to bail out.'

'Yeah, but... I should have—'

'Should have what?'

'Never mind.'

Faz hesitated. 'I thought you were dead, Dag.'

'I got thrown clear when Charlie crashed. So, you bailed out?'

'Yes. I did.'

A hush settled between them.

'Faz, the others...'

'I know. They didn't make it out, did they?'

Dag's voice was thick with remorse. 'No. I'm sorry. It's my fault. I killed them.' The confession hung in the air, uneasy and unresolved. 'But you're alive. And as long as I'm breathing,

I'll keep you that way.'

Faz regarded him, incredulous. 'Dag, look around you — we're in Normandy, hours beforea massive invasion. France is no sanctuary. Safe? None of us are safe.' He looked away, the longing in his voice unmistakable. 'I just want to get home. To see my wife. To hold my child.'

Dag nodded, conviction flickering in his eyes. 'Then I'll get you home. I promise.'

***

Bette saw it at once—the weight of guilt pressing down on him.

'You shouldn't have said that, should you?' she murmured.

Faz shook his head, regret etched into every line of his face. 'No, I shouldn't have. It just slipped out—like when you say, 'I wish I were somewhere else' or 'I wish I were home.' One of those things you never mean for real.'

'But for a man whose nerves were frayed, who never should've been flying, never should've been anywhere near a war zone—well, that was the worst thing you could have said, wasn't it?'

'That's not fair,' he protested, his voice tense. 'I was under pressure too.'

'Perhaps,' Bette replied softly, 'but you had the training. You ought to have known better. He latched onto what you said, didn't he?'

Faz stood abruptly, his anger barely contained. 'I don't need to listen to this, Bette. I think you should go.'

She rose too, matching his intensity. She hadn't realised how deeply this ran, hadn't even guessed. But she wasn't here to blame, not now; she needed the truth.

'I'm sorry,' she said, her tone gentler. 'Please, Faz, forgive me. Remember, I loved him too. I miss him—every single day. Please let me stay. Tell me the rest. After that, I'll leave.'

For a long moment, he hesitated. Then, with a resigned gesture, he motioned to the chair. She accepted the invitation and waited for him to continue.

***

Faz could see that Dag was alternating glances at the two German uniformed Poles with scanning the lane.

'What's the matter?' Faz whispered.

'I don't like the look of this,' Dag whispered back, nodding towards the guards. 'If I'm going to get you home, we're doing to need to do something.'

'Do what? We're prisoners. They have to treat us right. Remember, the Geneva Convention? None of our lads who've bailed out have had problems.'

'From the look on your face, Faz, I'd say the Jerries who took you in weren't too concerned with any convention.'

'That's true—they were SS. But these men? They're just regular Wehrmacht. Surely, they'll treat us as they would any other aircrew?'

'Faz, think. The crews that get to the camps may only be the ones that were lucky to be picked up by the right people. We don't hear about the ones who didn't. If I was in one of the cities we bombed, and a pilot came down and landed in the middle of a bunch of civilians I don't like to think what would happen.'

'Yes, but this is different. This isn't a town we bombed.'

Dag frowned and gave a little shake of his head. 'No, it's not. If anything it's worse. Think of what's happened to these guys already tonight and look at what's going on.' He looked up at the skies. 'This might be a diversion, but it probably isn't, this is the real thing, the invasion. If it is the day is only going to get harder to survive, this is all going to get bloody, one way or another. This pair know that. There's just the two of them, two of them and us at the moment. Their odds are better without us.'

Faz looked at the arguing pair. The younger one that had cradled and then dispatched the burning man, Jan, was the one being persuaded by his more belligerent colleague, who every now and then swung his rifle round to point at the two airmen, reminding them to keep still.

Faz realised Dag was right; this wasn't looking good.

'What do we do?'

'Make a break for it, find cover, make it hard for them to follow?'

'But they'll shoot us,' protested Faz. 'And with my leg I'm not going anywhere quickly. I'm hobbled.'

'Yeah, but look at them, Faz. These aren't front line soldiers, they're second rate. I bet they can't shoot for toffee.'

Faz stared at them. 'They're Poles,' he muttered. 'Every Pole I've come across is a decent shot.'

'Well let's hope these are the exception. Anyway, I'll drop behind, give them something to shoot at. That'll give you a better chance of finding cover.'

Faz looked at Dag in shock. 'But...you can't—'

'Look, Faz, I can, and I will. The rest of the crew — my crew — are gone. That's my fault, I ignored the recall signal.'

'It might not have been the recall, you said so yourself at the time.'

Dag shook his head. 'I was kidding myself. I wasn't thinking straight. It was, and both you and I know why. The CO was one call away from finding out I was LMF and shouldn't have been flying.'

'Yes, but...'

'But nothing. It might not have needed the call to my old squadron.'

'What do you mean by that?'

'Bette was there, remember. She didn't want me flying. She had a way to stop me.'

Faz stared at Dag in disbelief. 'Surely she wouldn't have done that?'

Dag shrugged. 'I don't know. I hope not but... Whatever, I've got no future back there. You have. Your wife is expecting. I'm getting you home, and that's an end of it.'

'No, Dag. Absolutely not.'

'Well, we've got to do something. Shit, they've decided.' Faz could see that both guards had nodded agreement and picked up their rifles. They turned towards the airman, the younger Pole pulling back the bolt on his Mauser to bring a cartridge into the breach.

'No time,' Dag, struggling to his feet, 'Faz, run, I'll take them.'

'No, Dag, no!'

Faz grabbed hold of Dag. Dag pushed him away.

'You just go. Go!'

The guard brought the rifle to his shoulder. Faz cowered away. It was all happening in slow motion, as if he was in a nightmare.

But this nightmare was all too real. Faz screwed his eyes shut, waiting for the end.

'Wait! Attendez! Nous pouvons vous aider à rentrer chez vous.' There was a long pause. Faz raised his head. Dag was facing off against the two guards. The first one still had the rifle raised but now looked uncertain. 'Vous n'êtes pas des Nazis. Ne faites pas leur sale boulot.'

Faz tried to work out what was being said, searching back through his pain-hampered mind to his schoolboy French. Dag was saying something about them not being Nazis, not to do their dirty work. Of course, they'd been based in France for years, they'd know the language.

'Vous n'êtes pas des tueurs. Nous sommes des camarades, n'est-ce pas?'

'Ya, camarades,' said the younger one. He reached out to his older comrade with the rifle. 'Lech, ma rację, nie możemy tego zrobić. Nie jesteśmy zabójcami.'

Lech shook his head. 'Ale się zgodziliśmy. Musimy się ich pozbyć.' He raised the rifle again.

'Non ! Regardez, c'est l'invasion.' Dag waved his hand towards the coast. 'Les Amis arrivent, aujourd'hui!'

Faz saw Lech glance in the direction Dag was pointing. He wondered what the point of saying this was. Wasn't this the reason that Dag himself had just advanced as to why the Poles would kill them? But then Dag's next line in his own schoolboy French explained his strategy.

'À la maison ! Tu ne veux pas rentrer ? En Pologne ? À Varsovie? À Dantzig? I mean À Gdansk?'

Faz realised. He was asking them if they'd like to go home. To Warsaw or Gdansk. His plan became clear. Time to help and try out his even worse Polish:

'Tak. Dom. Chodźcie z nami na plaże. Tommies. Amerykanie.'

'Ja, Amerykanie. Amerykanie,' said the younger one eagerly. 'The Americans. They come?'

'Yes, they do. Today!,' said Dag.

'You...want...us surrender?' he added haltingly in English.

'Yes,' said Dag. 'After you do something for us first. Nous avons besoin que vous fassiez quelque chose pour nous. Ensemble, nous pouvons y parvenir.'

Lech lowered his rifle. 'Mam nadzieję, że masz rację, Gustawie,' he growled. 'Très bien, Tommie, que veux-tu?'

***

Bette's eyes widened.

'That was a quick change about,' she said.

Faz nodded, smiling in reflection. 'Yes, Dag could think quickly when he needed to. And he did then. He saved us — saved me, I guess.'

Bette nodded. 'Yes. He could be quick witted when he wasn't being stubborn.'

'And persuasive,' said Faz.

Bette gave a rueful nod. 'So what did he want from the Poles? They were called Lech and Gustav, I take it?'

Faz's smile vanished. Bette wondered why. 'Yes, Lech and Gustav. He wanted an escort. To the coast.'

0112 HOURS
6TH JUNE 1944

This is a mistake, Faz thought. *What the hell are we doing? This is crazy.*

He looked at Dag walking alongside him. He seemed unconcerned, it was if he didn't have a care in the world. Faz wondered if he was in a dream, one of those weird ones where you found yourself doing something unbelievably stupid yet, for some reason, you had to go along with it and see it through to the end.

But if he was in this dream then Lech and Gustav were in it too. He looked back at them, their 'escorts', rifles slung over their shoulders following their two 'prisoners' down the road. Actually, this was barely a road, it was virtually a cart track, there was no tarmac, it was rutted, uneven, full of potholes. Although this meant it was unlikely they would encounter much traffic it also meant all of them stumbled from time-to-time, particularly when the moon went behind one of the scudding clouds.

It was bad enough for the rest but was particularly painful for Faz. His knee was not improving with the exercise; in fact it was getting worse. He had to keep his hand pressing down on his knee at each step to stop it collapsing, he could feel the heat and swelling through the fabric of his trousers. How long could he go on like this? It was agony, particularly when his foot plunged into a hole and was brought to a halt with a jolt.

It happened again. Faz stumbled but, this time, couldn't stop himself from falling.

'Fuck!' he exclaimed, crouching on the ground rubbing first his sore knee and then examining the damage to his hand caused by putting it out to arrest his fall.

'You all right, mate?' Dag put his arm around Faz. Faz shrugged it off.

'No, I'm bloody well not. This is mad, you must know that?'

'Mad? I thought you wanted to get home?'

'I do but…' Faz waved his hand around. 'Look where we are. It's bloody hopeless.'

***

'I expected Dag to yell back at me, to tell me to shut up and stop moaning but he didn't. He was surprisingly calm and understanding. He got me to the side of the road, sat me down, let me rest. The Poles were great too. One had some water with them. They gave it me, offered me a cigarette.'

Bette smiled. 'You're right, that doesn't sound like Dag as he was then. But, beneath all that bunch of nerves and pent-up anger that he was then was a decent, caring man. I saw it in flashes when I first met him. It could come out in the right circumstances.' She bit her lip. And, to her irritation, her voice cracked slightly when she added the coda: 'I'd like to have seen more of it in the future if he'd got back.'

Faz nodded. 'Yes,' was all he said. Bette guessed that was all he could risk saying without his own voice betraying him.

'Carry on,' she said. 'Finish your story.'

She was pleased that her tone had returned to normal. She was back in control.

***

Faz could feel the strength and his resolve returning to him as they sat by the side of the road. The night was still far from quiet; the drone of aircraft was ever present as was the crack of flak, the pyrotechnics that lit up the sky and the flash followed by the crump of detonations as the bombs landed but the belief that they could actually pull this off started to come back.

Dag was right. This was a chance. They were free. They'd

acquired a couple of allies, the Poles. If he wanted to see his wife and new baby anytime this side of the end of the war, then this was the way. Maybe it was a slight chance, one in ten? One in a hundred? A thousand? It didn't matter; it was a chance.

He listened as Dag talked to the younger Pole, Gustav who seemed to be keen in practicing his English, perhaps in preparation for the Tommies and GIs he expected to be meeting soon.

'Why are you working for the Nazi's?'

'Was? What?'

'The Nazis. Why shoot?' Dag leaned over and tapped the man's uniform and mimed bringing his rifle to his shoulder. 'Bang, bang. Why? The Nazis are your enemy.'

Gustav looked puzzled for a moment then said to Lech, smoking a cigarette next to him, 'Pyta, dlaczego tu jesteśmy. Why us here?'

'Yes, why? Twój kraj jest okupowany.'

Gustav nodded. 'Yes. Nazis come. Bad people. But Gustav told, you join army or you go to camp. Camp bad place. Bad food. Cold. Here better.'

'Fuck, you poor bastards,' said Dag, shaking his head. 'Come and fight for us or we'll lock you up, work you to death and starve you.' He looked at Faz. 'I know which I'd have chosen if I was in their shoes.'

'Me too,' said Faz.

***

Bette saw Faz close his eyes again. When he opened them, she could see there was a touch of moisture there.

'Dag was right. I'd have done the same too. Even though the consequences, the invasion, would, inevitably come at some point, I would have taken life in rural France over the alternative any day. Sure, they were in the military, ordered around, badly paid, treated like dirt but was still better than a camp. Gustav even had a French girlfriend; he showed us the picture.' He smiled. 'As well as the one he had back in Stettin.' The smile faded. 'Of course, he'd never see either of them again.'

'When did it happen?'

'About 15 minutes after we set off again.'

***

Dag suddenly put his arm out in front of Faz to stop him. Faz was about to ask what the problem was when Dag put his finger up to his lips. Faz nodded, he wasn't going to say a word. Dag turned around to the Poles behind him and made the same gesture. He then pointed down the road. Gustav frowned but then nodded, unslinging his rifle. Dag shook his head, but the Pole ignored him. He stepped out in front of the group.

'What is it?' whispered Faz.

'I saw someone down there,' Dag whispered back. 'They ran across the road. It looked like they were hiding.'

'Hiding? Not Germans then?'

'Probably not. They could be resistance or else paratroops. Gustav. Gustav!' Dag hissed. 'Come back!'

Gustav had started to walk down the road. He turned, about to speak, at the same time bringing his gun to his shoulder.

He never finished his action nor got the words out before the night was split with the bark of a Sten gun.

0131 HOURS
6TH JUNE 1944

Faz didn't stop, he ran; nothing mattered now; not Dag, not the Germans or the invasion, he was going to get away, to get home to his wife, to see his child when he or she was born. That was everything.

More shots. Lots of them, the sound overlapping like a deep cough.

'Toi ! Tu viens de la ferme. Ne tire pas!'

A brief pause. Then more shots. Shouting.

Abruptly he fell. Had he tripped?

Something was wrong. He managed to get to his feet again despite his trussed hands, but his right leg was useless. It wouldn't bear his weight, he fell, got up again but fell again.

Why? Sure, his knee was stiff after his landing, but he'd not hurt it any more since. Why had it suddenly got so much worse?

Whatever, he wasn't going anywhere. This was the end. He rolled on his back and stared up at the scudding clouds. The aircraft had magically gone; the sky was empty. He tried to picture his wife's face but just couldn't bring her to mind.

'I'm sorry, Sanaya, I'm sorry,' he whispered.

He was crying, actually crying.

This was how his life was to end was it; lying on his back in the dirt bawling his eyes out? What a failure.

'Faz, Faz, are you hit?'

Dag.

Was Dag dying too?'

'Shit, there's blood. He's bleeding. Have you got bandages? A medic kit?'

'No, we have not. Use the Nazi's clothes.'

A woman's voice. Who was she? A French accent, a young woman.

'They aren't Nazis: They're Poles.'

'They were in that uniform. That was enough.'

Reality abruptly returned. The woman *was* young, in her teens and he'd seen her before. She was holding her hand around Faz's knee. Now it hurt. He tried to push her off.

'Stop it,' she said, slapping his hands away.

'You. You were at the farmhouse.'

It was the farmer's granddaughter, but she looked very different now. The peasant dress had gone, she was now in men's clothes, rough, labourer's clothes, and her face was blacked up in soot or charcoal given that the rain had caused streaks to run through it.

And she was armed. She carried a Sten gun.

'Yes, I was.'

'You rescued us.'

'We did not intend to. He spotted us. We had to shoot. But there isn't time. Ve must get away. A patrol might come.' She looked over to her right. Faz followed her gaze. A man was bent over something on the ground, ripping, and tearing at the cloth that covered it. The light from the moon swept over them and the scene was revealed in stark detail; five men, dressed like the French girl, also with blackened faces and all armed with either rifles or Stens, held at the ready, stood in a rough circle warily watching the perimeter. In the centre of the circle lay a body, crumpled in an unnatural pose, uniformed, bloodied.

Gustav. It had to be Gustav. That was where he'd been standing.

There would be no after the war homecoming for him.

And Dag was leaning over him, pulling the man's shirt off and tearing it into strips.

He came over with his bundle of rags.

'Dag. What are you doing?'

'Here, let me get at it,' Dag muttered to the girl. She moved away a little. Dag looked into Faz's eyes. 'You've been shot. You got one in the leg.'

Shot? How could that be? From the range they'd been attacked from, a bullet would have taken his leg off. Maybe it had. Desperately he pushed the hands aside that were working to bind it.

'Faz, stop, we've got to stop the bleeding.'

Still, he fought until he saw that his leg below the knee was still there. Something had hit his calf. He lay back, relieved.

'A ricochet,' he muttered.

'Oui, you vere lucky,' said the girl. 'Eet has gone through.'

'Yeah, I really feel lucky right now.'

'Pardon?'

'Forget it. You need to bind it tight.' Faz advised. 'As tight as possible to stop the wound opening up.' He was pleased with himself; he was back in control of himself.

'Ok, I've got it.' Dag started to

'Bind it so it can't move, tighter, tighter,' Faz slumped back in pain. 'Where's Lech?'

'Dunno. I think he got away.'

'Good.'

'Is it? He won't be on our side anymore. He'll be looking for help.'

One of the men came over, looked down at their ministrations and shook his head.

'Putain, ça prend trop de temps ! Marie-Claire, nous devons y aller.'

Marie-Claire, that had to be her name.

'D'accord,' she replied.

'Laisse-les. Nous avons la mission à accomplir.'

'Je sais je sais!' The girl snapped back. 'Can you stand? Ve must leave now.'

'But—'

'It's all right, Dag, I'll give it a go.'

Faz struggled to his one good foot. That was fine. He gingerly tried to put the other leg down. The pain was like and electric shock.

'Faz, this is no good,' Dag said.

'It's fine, I can hop, if you can support me. Let's go.'
'But—'
'Let's go!'

0205 HOURS
6TH JUNE 1944

The anxious looks that Marie-Claire kept giving him and Dag told its own story; the pair of them, hobbled as he was, were falling behind.

Faz had tried, God he'd tried, it was like being back on the forced marches at the naughty boys' school in Sheffield. But it was hopeless, he was exhausted and the pain from his leg was excruciating.

'Dag, this is no good, we have to stop.'

'No, I have to get you somewhere safe.'

'There's nowhere safe, for God's sake man, see sense! Look around you, listen!'

Faz hadn't meant to snap but it had the desired effect. Dag stopped.

And the air force stepped in at just the right moment; the sound of engines, previously in the background rose until it drowned out everything else.

Faz jabbed his finger up at the sky. 'Sure, we've had this argument before which you won but look where that got us. They're bombers, Dag, ours, yes but that makes no odds, if we're anywhere near a target we're for it.'

The rapid flashes that lit up the sky a few miles away and the crump of explosions that followed a few seconds later proved his point.

'But still—'

Marie-Claire came back to them.

'Ve have to leave you, I'm sorry,' she said. 'It is the mission. We have our orders.'

'But—'

'She's right, Dag,' Faz said.

Dag nodded. 'Yes, I know'

Marie-Claire turned to leave but then stopped. 'You are both very brave. You good man, looking after your friend.'

Dag gave a ghost of a smile. 'I'm not sure about that,' he said, 'Good luck with whatever it is you're to do. Vive la France!'

She gave a little nod before vanishing again into the night.

Faz slumped to the ground. He inspected his leg. Of course, the wound to his calf had to be the same leg that he'd jarred on landing but then, thinking about it if it had been his other leg there would have no way he could have moved at all. To be honest it made no odds; the bandage was soaked in his blood, it was black in the moonlight. Whilst no artery had been hit, with him walking on it, even with the help of his makeshift crutch, was enough to keep open it up. It should have been cleaned properly too.

Dag sat down next to him. He'd been given a canteen of water by Marie-Claire, and he passed this to Faz who took it and drank from it.

'I'm sorry,' said Dag. 'I'm making a mess of things. Again.'

'It's not your fault. You didn't ask to be shot down.'

'No, but we shouldn't even have been where we were. That's my fault.'

'Dag, forget that. I don't blame you, neither would the others, but we must stop. We must surrender.'

'Surrender? How can we now?'

Faz frowned. 'What do you mean now? what's changed? We're still in the same place. we're still stuck in the middle of a war zone, one that's getting worse. There are armed bands of partisans everywhere, we're likely to find paratroopers if it's the invasion—'

'Which it is.'

'Yes, it probably is. So, we've got the resistance armed to the teeth on sabotage missions looking to kill. In a little while they'll be added to American, Brits and Canadian soldiers looking to take out the defenders and those self-same defenders trying their best to stay alive. Add to that we've got the RAF and USAAF prowling the skies looking to deliver tonnes of ordinance. And we're slap bang in the middle of it all.'

'Yes, we are, and that's exactly why we should go on.'

Faz stared at him in shock. 'Have you gone crazy? How the hell do you work that one out?'

'Okay, hear me out. Say we do manage to surrender, and that's not a given as everyone in a field grey uniform is going to have very itchy trigger fingers as you said. But if we do manage to find someone who does not shoot first and ask questions later, what happens then?'

'We're taken prisoner of course.'

'But taken where afterwards? I can tell you: some château or bunker, that's where. That's where we would have been taken if the truck hadn't crashed.'

'So what?'

'Think about it. You know how good the intelligence gathering has been. The invasion has been at least two years in the making. Two years of aerial reconnaissance, hundreds of thousands of photos. Add to that what the people on the ground like Marie-Claire have been reporting back. We only saw the tip of the iceberg as to what the top brass knows. You know what our and the 8th and 9th Yank air-force can do. So what are the first targets going to be? Those chateaus and bunkers, basically anywhere where senior officers and the Gestapo are. I don't know about you, but I'd rather be nowhere near anywhere like that.'

Faz felt himself weakening. There was some sense after all about what Day was saying,

'Alright,' he said. 'Added to that, if Bruno gets away from the resistance and tells his Polish mates what happened then they won't be on our side either.' He sighed. 'Damn it.'

'See. Faz, this is the way. I said I'd get you back to Soraya and your baby and I will, and keeping you out of the hands of the Nazis is the best way,' Dag smiled. 'Trust me'

'I did before. Right before I got shot,' grumbled Faz. 'But you're right, okay, we go on. But I'll need something to act as a crutch. A stout stick.'

'All right, I'll go and look for something,' said Dag. 'You rest there.'

Faz was left by the side of the road.
In the skies above the aerial armada grew ever louder.

0242 HOURS
6TH JUNE 1944

They'd made slow progress over the next half an hour or so. The night was lit up by flashes, fires could be seen in the distance, the low thud of the detonation of large bombs was their soundtrack, one that should have been alien but had become familiar and normal. It seemed that, despite their fears, no one would stop them because there were too many distractions. Who would be bothered about two airmen in enemy territory when so much else was happening? Faz began to believe Dag: this was, indeed, their best chance.

Dag saw them first. Faz was not surprised; his pilot had excellent vision. Like with the resistance before he stopped and, as Faz was being supported by Dag, Faz did too.

'What is it?' he whispered.

'Look,' Dag replied, pointing.

Faz strained to see. Two figures were making their way stealthily across the road in front of them. They vanished into the hedgerow.

'Resistance again?' whispered Faz.

'Maybe, Not Jerries anyhow, they were looking for cover. Could be paratroops, or downed air crew like us.'

'We should let them go, whoever they are,' warned Faz, 'I'd rather not get shot again, thanks very much.'

'Good point,' whispered Dag. They waited, eyes straining into the darkness. As it had been doing all right, the moon had gone behind a cloud. '

Have they—' Faz began but then heard something unexpected: the heavy thunder of hooves. 'What the...?'

In the distance came a shout: 'Mac! Look out! There's a bull!'

'Fuck it, run, Jonesy, run!'

Dag muttered 'They're Brits. Come on.'

'But Dag! Wait!'

But Dag had gone, forgetting that Faz was in no state to hurry: with his damaged leg, had no chance of keeping up. By this time, the thundering of hoofs had been joined by the bellowing of a bull and a crashing from the hedgerow.

Faz guessed that the desperate men had reached the hedge boarding the field and had tried to force their way through.

'Fuck! Fuck it! I'm stuck.'

'Hey guys, keep it quiet! You'll have the Jerries down on us!

That was Dag. His words were followed by a few moments of silence.

'Dag? Is that you?'

Faz knew the voice. It was Mackenzie, from their own Special Duties flight.

'It is. What are you doing here Mac?' Dag said.

'What it looks like. Being chased by a bastard French Bull of course! Jesus!' The Bull was still trotting angrily up and down the hedge bellowing. 'Christ, doesn't he know whose side were on?'

Faz had managed to catch up with Dag now. He could see Mackenzie had climbed up inside the hedge to get away from the angry bovine but was now tangled up in the branches and brambles.

'Hello, Mac,' he said.

'Hi, Faz. For God's sake, don't just stand there, the pair of you, damn well get me out of here.'

'Me too, boyos,' came a voice from their right. 'If you wouldn't mind awfully?'

***

'Were they both from your squadron?'

'Flight.'

She was momentarily put off balance. 'Pardon?'

'Special duties *flight*. Not a squadron.'

Bette looked at Faz in surprise. That was unusually pedantic for the normally polite Fazhad Khan. Why had he done that? Was he deliberately trying to distract her? Well, she wasn't going to be blown off course.

'Of course, a flight. I knew that. But the question still applies.'

'No, they weren't. Mac was, of course, he'd flown the repeat of the mission we'd tried to do the night before, albeit as just an arms drop rather than taking a Joe in.' Faz pulled a face. 'That carefully trained agent was, of course, buried in the Normandy countryside. Whatever, Mac had found the same flak battery as we had, he'd been a bit luckier, he'd got higher and reckoned all of his crew got out before he joined them taking to the silk.'

Bette nodded. She waited. Faz didn't show any sign of being forthcoming. Why? Was he being deliberately evasive?

'So who was the other chap?'

'Just some Dakota pilot. He'd been dropping a pathfinder party, and his bird had been winged. He'd bailed out too. He wasn't alone that night.'

Again, she waited. 'What was his name?' she asked at last.

She saw Faz hesitate.

'I can't remember.'

Bette's eyes widened. 'Really? I thought you had an excellent memory.'

'I do but, well, you must admit it's hard. It's been years and so much happened that night in such a short few hours.'

'You must remember something about him?'

Faz puffed out his cheeks. 'We just called him Jones or Jonesy. That's what Mac called him anyway. I never actually knew his full name.'

Bette stared at Faz. Was that the truth? Whatever, she was getting tired of this. 'I believe I can tell you it. Jones. Flight-Sergeant Daffyd Jones.'

Faz's eyes displayed a flash of alarm. 'How did you know?'

She smiled. 'I've been doing my own research. You must have known I would have.'

'Yes, I suppose so. Does that mean you know the rest of the story? Should I stop there?'

'No. I want to hear the rest. Carry on. Please.'

'The arguments started immediately,' said Faz. 'And it provoked Mac into saying something.'

'Saying what?' Bette frowned.

'Don't you know?'

'No, I don't.'

Faz raised his eyebrows at this but continued.

0300 HOURS
6TH JUNE 1944

'Our best bet is to go inland, see if we can meet up with the resistance or some of our SOE bods. We can then keep our heads down until the invasion comes through.' Mac nodded as if agreeing with himself.

'You can go that way,' said Dag. 'But we're heading west.'

'West? You're heading for the coast?' Mac pulled a face. 'If you're right about the invasion—'

'I am,' interrupted Dag.

'Then it's the last place to be,' Mac continued.

'That's what I keep saying,' said Faz. 'And he keeps talking me around.'

'How?' Mac looked at Dag. 'Explain your logic to me because I can't for the life of me work it out myself.'

They were sat under a tree on the other side of the lone from the field with the bull in it. Faz massaged his swollen leg whilst he listened to Dag repeat the same arguments as he'd listened to about forty-five minutes before.

'It's our best chance of getting back,' Dag concluded.

'It's our best chance of getting killed, more like,' said Mac. 'My plan is better. We meet up with resistance and wait it out until the invasion forces catch up with us.'

'If it gets that far,' muttered Jones. 'There's no guarantee that the lads will get off the beaches.'

'I won't have that kind of defeatist talk, Jonesy,' said Mac. 'The invasion will succeed.'

'We could still be here months, sir,'' said Jones.

'Got something pressing to get back for, sergeant?'

'No, sir. There's just me. Parents dead, no siblings, wife died in the Cardiff Blitz. No, all I have is me and I'd very much like to keep me from harm.'

'Well, this is the best way of doing that, Jonesy, believe me.'

Jones pulled a face. but shrugged. 'I think the longer we stay here, the more chance there is of getting caught and shipped off to a stalag. Me, I'd like to be a lot closer to home. 'He nodded at Dag. 'I think you've the right idea. I vote we head for the coast.'

'This isn't a democracy I'm afraid, Jones. I'll decide what to do,' said Mac.

'Not for me,' said Dag. We're heading for the coast. Right Faz?'

Before Faz could say anything, Mac had put his foot down.

'No, sergeant, as the senior officer here I can't allow it.'

'You can't stop us.'

'I can. I'm giving you an order,' snapped Mac.

'Sod orders. Rank means bugger all here.'

'Steady on, Dag, that's a bit much, ' said Faz. 'Sorry, Mac.'

'Don't apologise for me, Faz.'

'No don't. Let him dig his own grave,' said Mac. 'Anyway, we all know what you think about rank and authority now, don't we sergeant?'

'What do you mean by that?' Dag snapped.

'You were at the bad boys' school, weren't you? That was the gossip going around the base,' said Mac. 'Don't deny it because the CO had that radar woman in his office after you'd set off the other night.'

'What? ' said Dag. 'Bette was in with Ambrose?'

'Baxter, yes, that was her. The CO had a face like thunder when he came out. One of the Erks overheard some of it outside the office window. So why were you in Sheffield? Was it insubordination or LMF?' Mac demanded.

'None of your business,' Dag muttered.

***

Back in Faz's office, Bette went cold. Her heart fluttered, she felt suddenly lightheaded.

'Oh my God,' she muttered.

Faz's face was grim. 'I've never seen Dag look so shattered, so deflated. The fight in him evaporated.'

'But I didn't say anything,' said Bette. 'Yes, I was in your CO's office, and, yes, he demanded that I tell him what I knew but I said nothing.'

'Really?'

'Yes, really.'

'But a recall signal *was* sent?'

'Yes, it was, but not for anything to do with Dag. Both Squadron-Leader Ambrose and I were Bigoted, so we knew the landings had been delayed.'

Faz frowned. 'Bigoted?'

'It was the codeword for those who knew the time, date and place for D-Day, it was silly, the old way that mail for Gibraltar was labelled 'To Gib' reversed but it was effective. If you were Bigoted, you had special privileges, but you were also allowed nowhere near the continent. It was one of the reasons your CO was never allowed to fly on a mission even though, of course, Bomber Harris didn't like his commanders flying on ops, but we all know that was ignored. Ambrose didn't have a choice: He knew so it was an absolute bar. He'd have been cashiered if he had.' She paused. 'The forecast was bad, so it was scrubbed for 24 hours. We'd got the confirmation of the postponement, that was enough to stop the mission. As it was, we knew that there had been a security breach. You were all heading into a trap.'

Faz puffed out his cheeks. 'A trap that we waltzed right into.'

Bette nodded. 'So, Dag thought I'd betrayed him?'

Faz looked uncomfortable. 'Yes,' he said at last. 'We never talked about it, we never had chance, but it was obvious. He blamed you. I'm sorry.'

Bette stared at Faz. Sorry for what happened or sorry for

what Faz himself had told others since? This wasn't the time for confrontations. Not if she wanted to hear the full story.

'All right. What happened next?'

'Dag sat on his own. He looked lost in his own thoughts. The rest of us had a chinwag.'

'Had you all agreed to go with Mac then?'

Faz smiled. 'Not entirely. Jones was almost as awkward a character as Dag. It was like they were cast from the same mould, albeit one that was made in the Welsh Valleys.'

***

'How do we even find the resistance?'

'God above, Jonesey, enough!' Mac said in exasperation. 'This country is full of them. God, we should know, we've been dropping agents and arms for long enough.'

'Yeah, but it's also full of Jerries and informers,' Jone replied.

'The farmhouse where I was first held might be our bes bet to find the right people,' said Faz.

'Why do you say that?'

'The granddaughter, Marie-Claire, we saw there turned out to be resistance. She was part of the ambush that killed our escort. I think the old man was involved too.'

'Excellent,' said Mac. 'That's the plan then.'

'You can't go there.' They all looked in Dag in surprise. Faz for one thought he wasn't taking any notice of what they were saying.

'Why not, Dag?'

'Yes, why are you sticking your nose in?' snapped Mac. 'It's obvious you don't want to go there but the rest of us do so shut it.'

'It's not that.'

'Really? Pull the other one.'

'No, I mean it,' said Dag. 'Listen, we know the girl from the farmhouse was resistance because she was part of the party that ambushed and freed us.'

'So?'

'Faz, did Lech go into the farmhouse when the Jerries picked you up?'

'I don't...' Faz started then stopped. The guard that was eying up Marie-Claire. Was that Lech? The more he thought about it the more he was sure it was. 'I think so, yes. How did you know?'

'Lech tried to surrender and, when he did, he caught sight of Marie-Claire. He recognised her. I heard him.'

'Oh, come on. So what?' said Mac.

'It means we have a big problem if we go back there.'

'Why? I don't get it.'

Faz remembered, just before he was shot, what was said: 'Toi! Tu viens de la ferme. Ne tire pas!'

You're from the farm.

'He's right. One of the guards survived the ambush,' Faz said. 'He *did* recognise her.'

Mac pulled a face. 'Tough. It's a risk we'll have to take.'

'Oh, come on, we can't do that,' Dag protested.

'Yes, we can. We've taken enough risks for the resistance over the last year. They can do the same for us in return. How far is it? Do you think you could find it again?'

'It's not far, we left in a truck, but it came a cropper as did most of the poor sods in it.' Faz frowned, not wanting to be reminded of the Poles. 'If we just follow the road back, I should be able to recognise the track it's on. It can't be more than a couple of miles at the outside.'

'Perfect.' Mac checked his watch.

'Yeah, but a couple of miles on the road the roads the Jerries use,' Jones shook his head. 'We're going to fucking well get caught, I know it.'

'Jones. I've told you. Keep your trap shut. This is what we're doing.

'Nah, I'm going to the coast with your mate.'

'I'm not going to the coast.'

The other three looked in surprise at Dag.

'You've changed your tune,' said Jones. 'Why the switch?'

Dag pointed at Faz. 'I'm keeping him safe. I promised to get him back to his wife. She's due with their first. So, where he goes, I go.'

There was silence for a moment.

Then Jones broke it.

'Fucking English. Never could trust them.'

***

'So, did you make it to the farmhouse?'

Faz nodded but his look was a faraway one. 'We did. It didn't work out well.'

0403 HOURS
6TH JUNE 1944

'This looks like it,' Faz said. They were standing at the junction of the lane with the road, the former, barely a truck, led to a collection of farm buildings. which could barely be made out in the moonlight.

'It seems quiet,' said Mac.

'It is four in the morning,' said Jonesy. 'That's hardly surprising, is it?'

'No, I guess not. Still, it's a good sign. Let's go.' said Mac.

'Wait,' said Dag. They all looked at him in surprise. He'd not said a word since the argument with Mac.

'What is it now?' said Mac. 'Are you wanting us to turn around to protect your precious resistance woman?'

'Yes, but I know it's too late for that.'

'Then what's the problem now?'

'I just don't think it's a good idea for all of us to go mob handed. These are country folk. maybe the Jerries have taken their shotguns away, but what if they haven't, or they haven't found them all?'

'So?'

'So, I don't fancy having one shoved in my face by an angry Frenchman.'

'He's right,' said Jonesy, 'My folks were farmers and they'd not have taken lightly to being knocked up at this time, I'm not going anywhere near it until I know it's safe.'

Mac stared at them both. 'Hellfire, the pair of you were cut from the same cowardly cloth, weren't you? Sod you then, I'll go alone.'

Faz frowned. 'Do you speak French, Mac?'

Mac shook his head. 'Not a word.'

'Then I'll go with you,' said Faz.

'No, I'll go instead,' said Dag.

'No, you won't,' said Mac.

'But—'

'You'll flaming well do as you're told and stay here,' snapped Mac. 'I don't want you along.' He looked at Faz, resting on his makeshift crutch. 'You ready?'

'Yes. Let's go! He turned to Dag. 'See you soon.'

Dag gave a brief nod.

Faz set off with Mac, taking one last look at Dag sheltering with Jones the hedge at the start of the lane. Then he turned back and limped on.

***

Bette saw that Faz had closed his eyes again.

'The pain from my leg was intense. It was throbbing like hell,' he said. 'Maybe if it hadn't been I'd have been more with it. Maybe I'd have seen the signs. I don't know.'

***

Mac knocked softly at the farmhouse door. He listened. 'Bonjour. Hello?' He said then listened at the door. 'I think there's someone there,' he whispered to Faz. 'You speak the lingo. You have a go.'

Faz moved up to the door, but before he could speak it was opened from the inside. At the same moment came a shout from behind them.

'Halt. Hande hoch!'

Suddenly there were guns everywhere, all pointing at them. Faz was yanked inside the house so violently that he lost his crutch and was sent sprawling on the floor. There he received a series of kicks to the head and body. He rolled into a ball and put his hands over his head to try and protect himself, only to get a kick to his testicles that took his breath away.

'All right, all right, you've got us, for God's sake stop.'

Through his pain he was vaguely aware of Mac's protest.

'Wo ist das Mädchen? Où est la fille ?'

Over and over again this was shouted at them in different languages and, finally, in English. 'Where is the girl?'

An order was shouted. Faz didn't hear the actual words but, mercifully, the kicking stopped. It still took him some time to stop retching from the blow to his private parts.

At last, he felt able to move.

He rolled onto his back, panting, trying to take in what had happened. His face was swollen, one of his eyes was closing and the other was clouded with the blood that dripped down from a cut in his hairline, but he could see Mac propped up against the wall of the kitchen. Mac also showed signs of a beating. Rifles were still being pointed at them. Faz saw that one of the guards was Lech. He locked eyes with Faz then hawked up and spat in his direction. He grabbed his rifle and swung it towards Faz.

'Bękart!'

Faz flinched away as the gun's muzzle finished its trajectory.

The report of the round was deafening in the confined space. His ears ringing, it took a full second for him to realise he hadn't been hit. Looking up he saw Lech had been seized and that an officer was berating him.

'Du Idiot! Das Mädchen ist nicht da. Du hast uns verraten!'

'Er hat meinen Kameraden getötet.' Lech tried to spit at Faz again.

'Bring ihn weg!'

Lech was bundled out of the kitchen and outside.

'You all right, Faz?' said Mac.

'Never better,' Faz muttered.

'What was that all about?'

'He was one of the two Poles I told you about. He blames me for his friend's death.'

'God, I thought we had enough enemies as it was,' Mac muttered.

Faz looked around. Where were the farmer and his wife? Faz couldn't see any sign of them other than a suspicion looking pool of blood near the kitchen table.

The officer came over to them. Faz recognised him: he was the same Waffen-SS SS-Obersturmführer who'd been in charge of the patrol when he'd first been picked up.

'So, your friends from the resistance freed you, Sergeant? That itself shows you are not an ordinary aircrew,' he said.

'1838236, Khan, Fight-Sergeant.'

Faz received a punch to the face.

'You came back here? Why? Was this the agreed rendezvous? Speak, now!'

Faz said nothing.

The SS SS-Obersturmführer turned to Mac and screamed in his face.

'What was your mission? What was your aircraft?' he snapped in English. 'Talk!'

'1361529 MacKenzie, Flight-Lieutenant,' said Mac.

The SS-Obersturmführer shook his head. 'So, it's just to be name, rank and serial number is it. You will regret that when my colleagues in the Gestapo take over.' He looked at both of them in turn. 'Last chance, my friends. What is your mission?'

'1361529 MacKenzie, Flight-Lieutenant,' said Mac.

'1838236, Khan, Fight-Sergeant.'

'Very well. Take them away.'

A few seconds later Faz and Mac were back in the cellar where Faz had been only a few hours before.

***

'You were captured but Dag wasn't?'

'That's right.'

Bette frowned. 'So you were in the hands of the German's again? Yet you saw Dag again and reached Omaha?'

'Yes.'

'How?'

'I'll get to that part soon enough,' said Faz. 'You might as well hear the full story.'

0450 HOURS
6TH JUNE 1944

'Get your Goddamn hands off me, Kraut.'

'Hande Hoch!'

'Bewegen! Gehen!'

The farmhouse was suddenly filled with angry voices and tension. The cellar door was unlocked, and bodies blocked the light from behind.

There were soldiers being brought in, three them, all with faces darkened with black greasepaint, green battle fatigues contrasting with the Feldgrau of the guards. He didn't need to see a glimpse of the parachute badge logo on one of the men's tunics to know who they were.

Airborne! US paratroops.

Faz's heart pounded. He'd thought this the invasion, now he was certain. It was happening.

'Gehen! In! In!'

The tiny cellar suddenly got more crowded as three of the Americans were pushed inside. Two were huge, broad and burly whilst one, being supported by one of the others was tiny, a mere bantamweight. The latter was gently lowered to the floor.

'You sit there, Larry,' said the soldier who'd been supporting the little man. He turned to the other American. 'Sarg, Larry needs a medic. He's bleeding' bad.'

The sergeant went back up the cellar steps to the door and pounded on it. 'Medic! We need a medic in here. Now, goddamn it!' He looked through the keyhole. 'Hey, don't ignore me. Come back!' He moved away from the door. 'Shit.' He muttered. He looked at Faz and Mac for the first time. 'Who are you pair?'

'Faz Khan. RAF. I was shot down yesterday. This is Mac. Lieutenant Mackenzie.' Faz held out his hand, but the American sergeant ignored it.

'Yeah, 'course you are,' he said sneeringly. 'Kraut stool pigeons most like. What's the idea, Bud? Get us to talk because we think you're friendly faces?' He crossed his arms. 'I wasn't born yesterday. Kraut.'

Faz sighed. 'Have it your own way,' he muttered. 'We've got my own problems in case you hadn't noticed.' He slapped his bandaged leg. He looked down at the slumped man. 'What's wrong with your buddy? I've got some medical training.'

'Got one in the leg,' said the man who'd supported him. 'Didn't get a chance to look at it. Dropped right in the middle of a Kraut patrol. Damned snafu!'

Faz bent down. 'Let me look. Sergeant, can you move out of the way so I can get some light?'

Reluctantly the man did as he was asked. The light was still appalling but now Faz could see that the man's boot was at an odd angle. The leather of his boot had ripped suggesting the bullet had passed through it.

'His ankle's broken by the look of it,' he murmured.

'Can I help?' said Mac.

'Am I gonna lose it?' Even under the camo make-up, he looked pale.

'Naw, Kowalski, sit still. Let the medic look at it,' said his pal.

'Medic?' grunted the sergeant. 'Who heard of a limey kite carrying a medic?'

'They don't,' said Faz. 'I started training as a doctor in '40 which exempted me from war service, but I felt I needed to do my bit. Sure, I could have trained as a doctor with the army, I got the offer but I'd seen the aftermath of at the Luftwaffe did to Coventry, so I enlisted with the RAF. My father thought I'd gone mad.' Faz paused for a second and looked around the cell. He smiled grimly. 'Maybe he was right, come to think of it. Whatever, I was the navigator.' He looked up at his 'patient'. 'Kowalski, is it? I'll need to get your boot off. It's going to hurt

I'm afraid.'

Kowalski nodded but said nothing.

Faz looked up at Kowalski and Mac. 'Do you mind holding him. He's likely to move a lot and that could make things worse,' he muttered.

The American nodded and held out his hand. 'Kennedy,' he said.

Faz shook it as did Mac.

'Fighting' Irish?' Mac said.

Kennedy grinned. 'Too right.'

'Shut your mouth, Private,' growled the sergeant.

'Oh, come on, Sarg, he's helping.'

'Of course he is. He's wheedling his way in, bit by bit.' His arms remained crossed.

Kennedy shook his head. 'Forget him,' he whispered. 'What do you want me to do.'

'Hold his leg whilst I undo his boot.'

Kennedy nodded.

Faz started to gingerly pick and pull at the laces. Any slight movement of the boot hurt Kowalski, that much was clear.

This was going to take a long time.

***

'That was the first time you knew for sure that this was really the invasion?'

Faz nodded. 'It had been Dag that had been convinced but even after meeting up with resistance I'd always had a doubt. I thought what we'd been seeing could have been a diversion. Seeing real US airborne troops changed everything.' Faz smiled. 'I almost felt sorry for the Jerries.'

Bette frowned. 'Why?'

'Because here they'd been for four years, waiting in this quiet corner of France, getting soft with the butter, cheese and calvados, sitting in cider orchards canoodling with the local girls and suddenly, on this one night, that's all torn apart as the skies are full of aircraft, paratroops start landing all around them whilst the resistance blow up everything they can. Don't forget this was the early hours of the morning, hell we were shattered, dog-tired and on edge and it was obvious the Jerries were the same. Even the SS looked haunted, like they knew this day was the end.' The smile faded from his face. 'Thinking about it that explained a lot of what happened.'

**

It took a full twenty minutes before Faz sat back.

'How's he doing?' Kennedy asked looking anxiously at Faz.

'Kennedy, will you stop talkin' to that Kraut spy.'

The Irish American pulled a face. 'Sarg, I was just asking about Kowalski not spilling Uncle Sam's secrets.'

'Yeah, right. That's how it starts: get your trust, get you talking.'

Kennedy shook his head. He looked questioningly at Faz.

Faz couldn't see him well in the gloom, but Faz could tell Kowalski was bathed in sweat, his eyes were closed and breathing shallow. He could see the man's ankle. It was swollen to at least twice its normal size and was a livid purple.

'He needs proper treatment,' murmured Faz. 'The break needs splinting, and he needs morphine.' Kowalski opened his eyes and stared glassily at Faz. The latter made eye contact and smiled. The American closed his eyes again. Faz leaned back and whispered into Kennedy's ear. 'I'm worried about infection. The bullet split the bone. His marrow's exposed and there's dirt and cloth from his uniform in the wound. It needs proper cleaning and disinfecting.'

'What's he telling you?' said the sergeant. 'Don't listen to him.'

Kennedy looked at Kowalski then beckoned the sergeant over to the far side of the cellar where he started whispering something to his comrade. Faz realised he was repeating to the sergeant what he'd just been told.

'Great,' muttered the Sergeant glaring at Faz. 'So, what is it, Kraut? If we agree to talk our buddy gets treated. Is that your game?'

'No, it's bloody well not,' snapped Mac. 'Faz here is trying to help your buddy, can't you see that?'

The cellar lapsed into silence.

It was a minute before Kennedy broke it.

'Ignore him, he don't mean anything bad. It's just we'd trained for months for this and then it all went snafu right from the off.'

'I know,' said Faz.

'It wouldn't have if the damned fly boy piloting our ship had some guts and had kept going straight. Goddam chicken-livered, yellow-bellied loser.' The Sergeant shook his head. 'First sign of a few bullets and it all went to shit.'

'Flak and triple A?' asked Faz.

Kennedy nodded. 'It was like the fourth of July.'

'Can't blame your pilot then. At least we have armour, guns and self-sealing tanks. Those C47s have nothing.' Mac puffed out his cheeks. 'Coming in low and slow at night? No thanks, wouldn't do that for a watch as big as a frying pan.'

Kennedy pulled a face. 'I guess.' He looked at the door. 'I wonder where the rest of the boys are?'

The sergeant shrugged. 'Dunno. Probably in a POW camp by now. I guess that's where we're going.'

Mac gave a mirthless laugh. 'Eventually, maybe but only after having had a chat with the Gestapo.

Kennedy looked alarmed. 'The Gestapo? Why they wanna do that to us?'

'Because they know something big is happening and they'll want to know what's going on.'

Kennedy swallowed. 'We're prisoners. There's the Geneva convention. The got to treat us right, yes?'

Mac gave a snort of laughter. 'Supposedly, yeah, but don't count on it.'

Faz pulled a face. 'Come on, Mac, you know it's us they want to talk too. Kennedy, just ignore him.'

But he could see that Kennedy wasn't listening. His eyes were wide open now. He looked terrified. 'I didn't sign up for this. I'm getting outa here.'

He dashed for the stairs before anyone could stop him and started pounding on the door.

The sergeant and Mac were the first to react, hauling the frightened paratrooper away from the door and dragging him down the stairs. Kennedy fought back, struggling to free himself.

'Let me go! Guards, guards! I'll tell you everything. Just let me go!'

'Kennedy, shut it!'

'For Christ's sake, man, don't be an idiot,' Mac grunted. The pair of them managed to sit on Kennedy, pinning him down.

'Thanks, limey,' said the sergeant. 'First time in combat for these guys.'

The door was flung open and some of the guards, guns at the ready, entered and cautiously made their way down the stairs.

'Was machst du? Warum kämpfst du?' shouted one.

'Don't understand,' said the sergeant, shrugging.

The guard raised the butt of his rifle and struck him in the face.

'Ruhe! Nicht sprechen!'

'Bastard!' The sergeant reeled away, blood pouring from his nose. Kennedy took advantage of the situation squirm free.

The guard raised the gun butt again, but Kennedy beat him to it, scrambling across his comrade, trying to get out of the cellar. The first guard reeled back but the second didn't hesitate, clubbing the man to the ground with his rifle and hitting him twice more with the butt as he lay on the floor.

The sergeant tried to rise but Faz held him back. 'There's nothing you can do. You'll just get a bullet'

The sergeant seemed for a moment to want to ignore Faz but then sat back. Meanwhile the guards were picking up Kennedy, one on each side. Faz winced when he saw Kennedy's head. It was distorted; it was obvious his skull had been crushed.

'You'd better treat him right,' yelled the sergeant as they dragged Kennedy out of the cellar.

'I don't think there's much they can do to help him,' said Faz, as the cellar door was slammed shut and locked. 'He's not good. Not good at all.'

'Can't you two get your Kraut buddies to help him?'

'We haven't got any Kraut buddies, can't you sodding

well get that through your thick Yankee skull?' Faz couldn't help himself. 'Can't you see we're all in the same damned boat.' He drew breath. 'Sorry, I didn't mean to snap.'

The sergeant stared at Faz for a moment then gave him a grim smile. 'Okay, Limey. I'm convinced; you do sound real.' He held out his hand. 'The names Brewster. Sam Brewster.' Faz took it.

'Faz Khan.'

'John Mackenzie,' said Mac. 'Everyone calls me Mac though.'

'What's wrong with Kennedy? Is he going to be all right?"

'I think his skull is fractured. He needs a proper doctor.'

Brewster stared at the door in frustration. 'Shit. Has he got a chance? Is he going to die?'

'Probably,' said Faz. 'Sorry.'

Brewster shook his head and sighed.

'Ain't your fault. Still, if he's dead he can't shoot his mouth off to the Krauts.'

Faz pulled a face. 'That might not help you with our date with the Gestapo. Kennedy's little outburst is going to get reported. That means you'll definitely get interrogated now too.'

'Damn, you're right,' said Brewster. 'Kennedy. You've really dropped us in it, buddy.'

0525 HOURS
6TH JUNE 1944

The key rattled in the cellar door again and it burst open.

'Raus! Raus!' screamed the guard. 'Out, out!'

'Looks like this is it,' said Mac. 'Do you need a hand with Kowalski?'

Brewster shook his head. 'No, I can manage. You help the doc. Come on, Bud.' The sergeant pulled Kowalski to his feet.

'What is it? Where are we going? Let me sleep,' muttered Kowalski.

'We've got to go.'

'Raus! Raus!'

'All right, we're coming.'

Mac glanced at Faz as he put his arm around the navigator and pulled him to his feet. 'I wonder where they are taking us.'

'Nicht sprechen!'

The four men emerged into the kitchen. The sound of an engine could be heard, something heavy was bumping down the track towards the farm. Faz guessed it was another truck.

'The local Gestapo headquarters probably,' Faz whispered to Mac.

The SS SS-Obersturmführer was at the farmhouse door peering out into the dawn light. He turned back to the two airmen and the two Americans. 'Your transport is here. One last chance to talk. Do it, now!'

'Go fuck yourself,' said Brewster, struggling a little to keep Kowalski upright.

The SS-Obersturmführer wore a sardonic smile as he

walked up to the American sergeant. 'Such tough talk, cowboy,' he said. 'Maybe you can stand up to the Gestapo. Do you think your comrade here can do the same?' He raised his boot and pressed it down on Kowalski's broken ankle.

The man screamed, jerking upright.

Both Faz and Mac attempted to get free and intervene, but both were held back. The SS-Obersturmführer laughed.

'Nimm sie raus,' he said to the guards.

They were herded out into the farmyard. Faz could see it was getting light, the sky now an eggshell blue, the clouds tinged with pink. This was it, the day everyone had waited for so long.

And he was going to miss it.

The truck was just pulling into the farmyard. Faz guessed that the Waffen-SS officer had radioed for it, having given up on the idea of ambushing Marie-Claire and the rest of the Maquis: either they were busy elsewhere or Lech's shot having given the game away. Whatever, their transport had arrived.

The guards pushed them forward. One of them stepped up to the cab, clearly intent on speaking with the driver.

A single shot rang out. The guard staggered back, half turned and then fell.

'Scheisse!' said the Obersturmführer ducking for cover back into the farmhouse.

He was almost alone in reacting. The rest of the guards were momentarily frozen, the shock clear on their faces as their sleep-deprived brains tried to process what was happening to them.

It was a fatal delay.

Bodies poured from the back of the truck. They started shooting, picking off the guards. The one holding Faz let go of him and tried to run but was cut down after taking two steps by a burst of fire from a Sten.

All over the yard men were now running or trying to fight back. It was hopeless, an elite unit or not, they had been taken by surprise. Many were falling, dying. Some tried to surrender, to no avail. They were shot as they knelt in the dirt. A couple of men walked past Faz and went into the farmhouse, even with the camouflage paint on their faces he recognised them: they were part of Marie-Claire's partisans the same ones they had been with a couple of hours before.

Amid the shouts and muffled shots emanating from within the building, Faz was suddenly grabbed and hugged so tightly he could barely breathe.

'You're all right! My God, you're all right.'

***

Bette stared, open mouthed at Faz.

'Dag? It was Dag? He came with the resistance?'

'Came? He was virtually leading them. He had a revolver, he had his face blackened, his eyes were wild. It was like I'd not seen him for a year rather than just a few hours.' Faz puffed out his cheeks. 'It wasn't the time to analyse him, not after what had just happened — was still happening in fact.'

Bette nodded. 'But later you did?'

'Yes. I was always interested in the mind. I once thought I'd specialise in psychiatry before I decided to be a GP.'

'So what was your diagnosis, doctor?'

Faz shook his head. 'There wasn't enough evidence to do that.'

'Rubbish.'

'But—'

'I'm sorry, Faz but with respect, this wasn't the only time you'd seen it, was it. You'd known him for months. He'd become a friend, yes?'

'Yes.'

'And you'd seen him at his worst and best. So, tell me what you saw and what you thought.'

Faz stared at his desk for a few moments. Then he nodded as if he was confirming something in his own mind. 'That night — morning really — at the farm, he was himself but a self that was Dag amplified, sped up, talking ten to the dozen.' He smiled. 'That was so unlike Dag.'

Bette also smiled, albeit briefly 'Yes, he wasn't one of life's great conversationalists. So…?'

Faz was silent for a moment, perhaps reluctant to speak

what was in his mind, Bette decided. She was about to tire of it, tell him to forget it, to move on to what was important to her: hearing the story but Faz chose to speak.

'He was manic. I'd thought I'd seen the signs before; the mood swings, the switching between dark moods and elation, of periods where he could sleep the day away to insomnia and bouts of nervous energy. It was more than just stress, it was clinical. If someone in my practice came to me presenting those symptoms I wouldn't hesitate to make a referral.'

'A manic-depressive?'

Faz nodded. 'Yes.'

Bette took a deep breath. 'That makes sense. So he should have had treatment back then?'

'He should. But the treatment is brutal. Electric shock therapy. Confinement. It might have made it easier for others but not for the patient. But still, I knew it then.'

'And perhaps even before then?'

Faz looked grim, troubled. She'd pushed him too far.

It was time to move on.

'That's all immaterial now,' she said. 'What happened next?'

***

'Bloody hell, Dag, I didn't know you had it in you.'

Mac had stood back whilst Dag had sought out Faz but had now stepped forward.

'It wasn't me. It was Mademoiselle Beaumont and her friends that did all the work. I just went along with it. Believe me, I was scared to death. Mind you I prefer this to facing flak and fighters. At least you can see who the enemy is.'

Dag's words tumbled out in a rush.

Mac frowned for a moment then held out his hand.

'I think you're being modest. It was bloody brave. I'm sorry, I can see the CO was wrong about you. I'm going to put in a good word for you when we get back. I'm sure this will swing it.'

Dag took the hand and shook it.

'Thanks, Mac.'

The shots from the house had stopped but, abruptly, a

woman's scream rent the night.

'What the…?'

'That's Marie-Claire,' said Dag. He ran into the farmhouse.

Jones hopped down from the back of the truck. He walked over to Faz and Mac and the two Americans. 'You boyos okay?' he said and then puffed out his cheeks. 'Hell, I don't want to go through that again.'

'What happened,' said Mac. 'Where did the resistance come from. How did Dag find them?'

'He spotted them coming back. They'd been on a sabotage mission.' Jones looked at Faz. 'Apparently you'd run across them before?'

'Yes, that's right. They freed us.'

Jones nodded. 'Dag's eyesight and hearing are damned impressive. He heard them coming then spotted where they were. I had no idea they were there but once he pointed them out, I was all for laying low and letting them past but, no, Dag wasn't having it. He broke cover and went right up to them.' Jones shook his head. 'How they didn't shoot him, I've no idea but he was determined that they wouldn't walk into the trap.' Jones grinned. 'And, once he'd done that, he then persuaded them that to lay their own ambush.' Shouting could now be heard from the farmhouse. A woman's voice. 'What's going on?'

'Let's see,' said Mac. He went into the house, Faz and Jones followed.

A strange tableau was laid out. The kitchen was splattered with blood, a couple of dead SS men were being searched by the partisans. Three live Germans were on their knees, their hands tied behind them, covered by the guns of the rest of the resistance fighters. One was the SS-Obersturmführer. Everyone was staring at Marie-Claire who, pistol out, was being held by Dag. Her face was pure fury; her camo make-up streaked with tears.

'Let go, let me at zem,' she yelled.

'What is it?' said Mac.

'They killed her grandparents,' said Dag. 'When they first got here. Shot them in cold blood, in the back of the head.'

'Bâtard!' Marie-Claire still struggled. 'Let me at him.'

'Mademoiselle Beaumont, please,' said Dag. 'I know you want revenge, but you can't execute him.'

'I can! Watch me.'

'Yes, I know you can but this isn't like killing someone in combat. This would be murder. You'd have to live with yourself afterwards.' Dag smiled. 'I know that feeling only too well. I've killed, yes in combat but I know I've killed the innocent as well as the guilty. Don't fall into that trap.'

Marie-Claire struggled for a few moments then Dag's words seemed to hit home. 'All right,' she said.

Dag let her go. 'May I have your pistol?' he said holding his hand out. 'Just in case.'

Marie-Claire handed it over.

'Thanks,' said Dag. He turned to the Waffen-SS Leutnant. 'I, of course, am already living with my conscience so…'

To Faz's horror Dag brought the pistol up to the man's head and pulled the trigger.

LECIESTER
MARCH 1951

Bette got to her feet and went and looked out of the window. It was getting dark; the streets of Leicester soaked with the rain that had fallen steadily all day. What she saw held no interest for her: She hadn't come to the window to look out but to try and work through what she'd just listened to.

Faz obviously sensed her distress.

'Are you all right, Bette? Can I get you something? Tea? Something stronger?'

She shook her head. 'No, I'm fine.'

She knew that was far from the truth. Still, she forced herself to return to her seat in front of Faz's desk and sat back down again. Faz had also risen but joined her in sitting.

Bette swallowed. She needed to get this over with. She had to get Faz talking again, if only to smooth her jagged nerves.

'How did everyone else react?' she said.

Faz shrugged. 'I guess we were all shocked. Marie-Claire was already distraught. She'd lost her parents after all. Dag...' Faz stopped. Bette frowned. Why had Faz hesitated there? Before she had time to think it through, Faz had picked up the thread again. 'Whatever, that wasn't the time to discuss it. We were on the farm with a dozen dead Germans, some of them Waffen-SS to boot. They didn't exactly have a reputation for being forgiving. We had to get away, smartish, before any reinforcements arrived.'

Bette nodded. Then frowned.

'There were other prisoners. What happened to them?'

'Don't worry. They were just trussed up and left there. The French wanted to take them out and shoot them, but Mac insisted that they weren't harmed. Yes, it may not have been wise, they could have identified us and Marie-Claire, but Mac demanded that they be left.'

'So, where did you go?'

0610 HOURS
6TH JUNE 1944

The resistance group led them across fields and down farm tracks away from Marie-Claire's house. The Americans and the British aircrew hadn't been told where they were going, Faz presumed it was to another resistance house to lay low. Faz was being supported by Mac, whilst Brewster was carrying Kowalski, the bantamweight airborne soldier's head lolling to one side. Faz guessed that the pain from the mans shattered ankle had got too much and he'd fainted. Though his burden was light, Brewster was puffing as he laboured under his comrade's weight. There were shades of a few hours before when Marie-Claire had kept looking back as Faz had struggled to keep up. This time Marie-Claire was walking with Dag who she'd seem to have formed a bond with, she was still clearly distressed, too distressed to worry about them: Now it was other members of the resistance who anxiously glanced at them and urged them to hurry.

Faz knew they couldn't. This was impossible. He waited for the next glance back and, when it came, he stopped and shook his head. The resistance man looked irritated, he waved them on, but Faz shook his head. 'Rest' he mouthed. The man's irritation increased but he nodded. There were whispered orders, and the caravan stopped.

Mac gently lowered Faz to the ground, then helped Brewster with Kowalski. As Faz had guessed, the little American was out of it. He was worryingly pale, and his breathing was ragged.

'He's not good, is he?' murmured Brewster.

'No, he's not,' said Faz. 'I think he's gone into shock.'

Marie-Claire had gone with Dag to talk to the resistance men. Jones settled himself down next to Faz and Mac.

'You boyos all right?' he said.

'Not really,' said Faz. 'We're holding everyone up. We did before when it was just me.'

'That can't be helped,' said Mac.

'It can. You're not going to get far with Kowalski and me. Leave us. I'll look after him.'

'Not a chance, Bud,' growled Brewster. 'I ain't leaving him.'

'And I'm not leaving you,' said Mac. He looked at Dag, talking with Marie-Claire and the resistance men. 'Particularly as wherever you are, he'll stay too.'

'What's the problem with that?' said Faz.

'I don't trust him,' Mac said, casting glances at Dag and Marie-Claire.

'You've changed your tune,' said Faz frowning. 'I thought when he organised the rescue, he was the bee's knees.'

'That was before I saw him execute a prisoner in cold blood.' Mac's eyes fixed on Faz. 'You can't say you weren't shocked by that? That you condone it? Well, do you?'

Faz glanced at Dag.' No, I don't. But...'

'But what? You've studied medicine, haven't you?'

'Yes.'

'Psychology?'

'Yes.'

'So what's your diagnosis, *doctor*?'

***

Bette couldn't help but smile at this, despite the grimness of the story. She'd used pretty much the same words to Faz a few minutes before.

She didn't interrupt though. She needed to hear the rest of the story.

***

Faz was about to argue that he wasn't a doctor, but it seemed pointless. 'All right, I don't think he's well, mentally I mean.'

'Exactly,' said Mac triumphantly. 'It's what I said: He's a danger to everyone, himself included. I'm guessing that's why he was at the bad boy's course.' He glanced at Dag, then leaned forward to whisper to Faz. 'When we get back, I'll be reporting just that to the RAF.'

Faz stared at Mac in disbelief. 'You can't do that.'

'Doing that is better than the alternative. It's either that or I'll say he's mentally sound and report him for killing a prisoner. Either way he's finished.'

'You can't do that to him. Please, Mac.'

'Please Mac, what?'

Both men looked up in surprise at Dag who neither had noticed had come over.

'Nothing,' said Faz quickly, glaring at Mac. To his relief Mac kept quiet. 'What's the verdict?'

'It's the same problem as before. We're holding them up. They need to get to safety. They would like us to split up from them. I have to say they're right. If the invasion goes wrong, they'll be hunted. They've more chance on their own.'

Mac scowled. 'So, they're going to leave us? Great.' He looked back in the direction of the farm which they left not 30 minutes before. 'It's quiet now but it won't be too long before the Jerries go looking for their missing men. Then they'll be hell to pay.'

'It was you who insisted on keeping those guards alive,' said Dag.

Mac stared at Dag in astonishment. 'You wanted to commit more murders? You really are crazy.'

'I'm a realist. Your ideals will get us killed.'

Mac got to his feet. 'I outrank. you, sergeant.'

'Yes. Sir,' Dag and Mac were now face to face.

'Come on, stop it, the pair of you,' said Faz. 'This isn't helping.'

'Did I ask you to put your oar in? and you can call me sir, too, sergeant.'

'Hellfire, what are you Limeys like? I thought you were all tea-sipping gentlemen, passing the cucumber sandwiches around,' said Brewster. 'When really you fight like rats in a bag like the rest of us.'

This seemed to break the spell. 'Sorry, yes, quite,' muttered Mac. 'So, what's the plan? Let the Frenchies go and leave us here?'

'Not quite,' said Dag.

'What do you mean by that?'

Marie-Claire came over to them. 'Are you ready?' she said.

'Ready for what?' Mac stared from one to the other, but Dag was already with Brewster.

'I'm sorry,' he said. 'We can't take you. We'll have to leave you here, Kowalski's in no state to move, hope you understand?'

'But... What are you up to, Sergeant? Where are the rest of us going?'

'To the coast, of course,' said Dag. 'Marie-Claire has agreed to help us.'

'About time,' said Jones. 'I'm in.'

Mac stared at Dag. 'No. Absolutely not. For God's sake, we've had this argument before. I vetoed it then and I'm doing the same now.'

'You don't get a say. This is the best way to keep us out of a prison camp. Or worse, in fact, given what happened back there. They'll be after our blood.'

'It's the best way of getting us killed. It was before and it is now.' Mac Folded his arms. 'We're not doing it. Absolutely not.'

'Things have changed.'

'No, sergeant. It's not happening.'

To Faz's horror, Dag pulled out his revolver. 'Yes,' he said. 'It is.'

***

'No.' Bette shook her head. 'I don't believe it. Dag really did that?'

Faz raised his eyebrows. 'You seem to be more shocked about that than the fact he executed a prisoner.'

Bette had to think about this before replying. Faz was right; she was more affected by hearing this. She tried to work through her thoughts. 'Yes, I suppose I am. His executing that SS man made some sense. He had been responsible for murdering that French girl's — '

'Marie-Claire,' Faz interjected. Bette frowned. Why was the girl's name relevant? She tried to dismiss it, but she couldn't. It niggled at her so much that, for a moment, she lost her thread. She forced herself to complete her thoughts. 'Yes, quite, Marie-Claire, her grandparents. He was both the enemy and a killer. I could understand that. But putting a gun in the face of an RAF officer, there's no excuse for that. Why did he do it?'

Faz took a few seconds to reply, she could almost see the conflict raging within him between Doctor Farzad Khan the physician and Faz Khan the friend of Douglas Atkinson-Grieve. It seemed that the doctor inside won.

'Where you have cases such as Dag's, when they are in a state of mania the decisions they make are not illogical or insane but tend to be merely extreme. It's as if both the thought processes are speed up and all normal boundaries of reasonableness removed. According to Dag's thinking the best way for us...' He paused. '— me I suppose — to survive was to get me away from the vicinity of the farm where they'd be a good chance we'd run across some vengeful SS men who'd have no compulsion about killing us out of hand in revenge. That meant doing one of three things: hiding out and waiting in the hope that the invasion forces would reach us before we were caught, which, as we know now, would have meant hiding for months not days or even weeks; heading further into France and, perhaps, joining up with the resistance and getting to Spain; or and I can understand this logic, heading for the coast in the knowledge that there at least we'd have friendly forces within reach.' Faz smiled. 'The mania drove Dag to quickly select that as the best option, even though it seemed crazy and entailed huge risks, it was actually less risky than any other course. Once he'd decided that was what we needed to do then that was it. He wouldn't let anything get in his way in going through with his plan.' He tapped his fingers on the desk.

'Anything or anybody.'

Bette nodded. 'So, what did Mac do? Come with you?'

Faz shook his head. 'No. He stayed with the Yanks.'

***

Mac watched as Jones, Faz, Dag and Marie-Claire prepared to leave. The resistance men had gone through their kit and given a couple of ancient revolvers to Faz and Jones and the pair of them were stowing these and the few rounds of ammunition the French had been able to spare.

Once they were done Mac quietly gestured to Faz to come over.

'Faz, please don't do this. He'll get you killed.'

Faz shook his head. 'Sorry, Lieutenant, I'm going.'

'Then on your head be it. Listen carefully, Khan. If by some miracle you make it, which I very much doubt I'll expect you to make a report on what's happened tonight to the RAF. A full report. I know I will be making one which will detail everything that's happened tonight. It will be bad for you if your report differs from mine. Do I make myself clear?'

Dag nodded. 'Perfectly clear, sir,' he said. He glanced at Dag, in conversation with Marie-Claire. He swallowed. Dag's career was over, that was clear, if they got back. Would his own be too if he didn't tell the truth?

***

'Why did you go along with it? You could have refused. And why did Jones go along with it? Couldn't he see that there was something wrong with Dag.'

'Jones seemed not to care. He'd lost his wife and just seemed fatalistic, as if he was convinced that nothing could happen to him, that he'd survive, whatever.'

'Which he did.'

She saw Faz swallow. His throat seemed dry. 'Yes, he did,' he said.

'All right, you've said that Jones was almost as bad as Dag. But what about Marie-Claire? What about you? You

103

certainly had a hell of a lot to live for, didn't you?' Bette pointed at the picture of Faz's wife and children. 'Why didn't you tell him to go to hell? And this Marie-Claire, she was young, what age was she by the way?'

'Seventeen. Nearly Eighteen.'

'Old enough to know better and an experienced fighter?'

'Yes.'

'So why did she go along with it?'

Faz hesitated. 'I don't really know. She'd been living with her grandparents because her father had been shipped off to work for the Germans somewhere. Her mother was dead. Perhaps she saw Dag as a big brother, I really don't know.'

Bette couldn't hide her surprise. 'You seem to know a lot about her. You didn't spend that long together, did you?'

'Long enough.'

Bette waited but nothing else was forthcoming.

'So why did you go along with this crazy plan?'

Faz grimaced. 'How could I not? with Dag in that mood? Look, I wanted to make sure Mac got out of there in one piece. To do that I had to make sure he and Dag were separated. As Dag would go where I was then we had to go along with his plan.'

'It was that bad?'

'Yes. It was. And it immediately became clear how bad it could be.'

***

They had gone less than a few yards before, abruptly, the sky lit up. Not to the east where the sun was just rising, but to the north. At the coast.

The flashes were eventually accompanied by the soundtrack. A steady rumble, like thunder but thunder that never stopped. It just went on and on.

No one said a word. They all knew what it meant. They just walked on towards the sound of the guns.

0712 HOURS
6TH JUNE 1944

All three airmen looked up as a flight of twin engined bombers hurtled towards them at low altitude, the early morning resounding to the sand of the thundering radials.

'Yanks', observed Jones. 'Marauders.'

As they watched the Marauders bomb bay doors opened revealing their load of green painted 500lb bombs within.

'Somebodies going to get it,' Faz murmured. 'I almost feel sorry for the Jerries.'

'I do not,' said Marie-Claire. 'Boche bastards. They deserve everything they will get.' She spat on the ground to add an unnecessary emphasis to her words.

'Yeah,' said Dag. 'Quite. Did you see the black and white stripes. Wonder what that's all about.'

'We were ordered to paint them on our kites overnight,' said Jones. 'It was all hands to the pump. Even the Wingco was out there with a paintbrush.' Jones grinned. 'Mind you he was rubbish. I could see why he'd been kicked upstairs.'

More Marauders sped over them. Faz could see one of the waist gunners leaving out of his position, his 50-calibre gun still to hand. He gave a laconic wave as the Martin machine passed the small party.

Then the sounds of bombs could be heard falling. The aircraft were so low that they didn't fall for long. The sounds of detonation and the and the blast wave reached them almost simultaneously. Faz felt his ears pop with the changes in pressure. He covered them with his hands to protect them from the noise and to reduce the risk of the pressure damaging them. He saw the others, including Marie-Claire, doing the same. They all crouched down together, waiting for the storm to pass.

At last, the detonations stopped, and the sound of the aircraft's engines started to recede.

Dag cautiously got to his feet and peered in the direction of where the bombers had attacked. 'It looks like it's over,' he said.

Faz joined him. All that could be seen was smoke rising from a spot a couple of miles distant.

'What do you think the target was?' he said.

Dag shrugged. 'I don't know. Could have been a railway, a road junction or some command centre. At least it wasn't us. We need to get on.' He scowled as he scanned the landscape that lay ahead of them. 'It looks like there's another one of those damned ditches ahead of us. How many more of them will we have to cross?'

Faz nodded. The flat ground made progress relatively easy, and the hedges gave them a decent amount of cover, but they'd now come across an area which was cris-crossed with drainage ditches, many of which were filled with water, recently refreshed by the rain from the day before.

'Eet is like this everywhere around here,' said Marie-Claire. 'Eet is low lying. It floods.'

'Well, it's a damned nuisance, whatever the reason,' grumbled Dag

'How far have we got to go?' said Jones. 'Where are we?'

'From memory based on some of the trips we did, I would say near Mandevellie-en-Bessin, I think,' said Faz. 'Is that right, Marie-Claire?'

'Oui, that is correct.' She pointed towards the west. 'Over there is Trévières. Eet is a big place. There are many Boche there.'

'So about 5 miles to the coast?'

'Oui.'

'So, just over an hour. Normally that is,' said Faz.

'But this isn't exactly normal, is it?' said Jones. As if to confirm his words the sounds of gunfire increased. 'It sounds like all hell's broken loose over there.'

'The quicker we get there the better,' said Dag. 'We'll have to risk the road.'

The others looked at him in shocked surprise.

'But you are in uniform. Eet is light,' protested Marie-Claire.

'It is but the Jerries are too busy keeping their heads down. And we'd be able to hear anyone coming and make ourselves scarce.

'But—' Faz began, but Jones cut him off.

'Dag's right,' he said. 'I'm sick of trying to cross these stinking ditches. It's going to take all day. Come on, let's find that damned road.'

***

Bette nodded to herself. 'I'm beginning to see what you mean. There's some logic there. Twisted logic but logic nonetheless.'

Faz gave a little laugh. 'Logic yes. Albeit one with a considerable snag.'

'What was that?'

Faz smiled. 'It wasn't exactly a quiet walk in the countryside.'

0805 HOURS
6TH JUNE 1944

The roar came out of the blue, the three airmen and the French girl all instinctively flinched.

Blat! Blat!

Two Spitfires IXs, empty bomb shackles under each wing flashed low over them in a blur of camouflage marred with the dramatic bold black and white stripes, their Merlins straining at full throttle. The aircraft were at treetop height, so low that they'd not heard them coming, hence the almost visceral shock of their arrival and the abruptness of their immediate passing.

Faz felt his heart thumping in his chest, the acrid taste of fear in his mouth. Judging by the look on everyone else's faces, they all felt the same. Even Dag had gone white.

Jones puffed out his cheeks.

'Bloody hell,' he said. 'I almost pissed myself. Where did those boyos come from?'

Faz and Dag exchanged glances. Faz could see that Dag knew they had a problem. A big problem.

***

'It was the noise. There was so much of it. The sound of fighting from the beaches. The crump of shelling which, I know now, were the battleships bombarding the area behind the beachfront' He paused. Bette could see he was back in the moment, remembering. She said nothing, not wanting to interrupt the flow. 'Then there were the bombers,' he said. 'The heavies. They kept coming. Boy, did they keep coming.'

***

'Ve should get off the road,' Marie-Claire muttered. 'Ve cannot 'ear anything.'

Faz nodded. 'She's right, Dag, we'll never hear anyone coming. A whole bloody pack of Tigers could turn up and we'd never know — what the hell?'

They all looked to the left of the lane. About 200 yards ahead of them, behind a small copse on the left side of the road, the thud, thud as artillery piece opened up. At first it was just one gun, but others rapidly followed.

The four looked at each other, momentarily frozen in fear.

'An anti-aircraft battery. Eighty-eights! My God, we almost walked right into them,' Faz said.

'Get off! Get off the road!' Dag urged.

There was a gap in the hedgerow on the right. The group hurried through it and hid behind the hedge as the barrage continued. High above them the drone of a bomber squadron could be heard. Faz squinted up into the early morning light, shielding his eyes. He could see the aircraft now, four-engined machines. The flak was bursting all around them.

'Yanks?' said Jones.

'In daylight it has to be. Fortresses or Liberators,' said Dag. 'Shit, they've got one!'

Faz's heart thumped as he watched the bomber, shedding parts, bank away from the formation. Black dots fell away from it.

'He's jettisoned his bombs,' said Dag. 'Oh God...'

Almost right above them, the aircraft, Faz could now see it was a Liberator with its long slender wings and twin tail, twisted into a violent spin as one wing came off.

'Jump, jump!'

It was hopeless, he knew. He'd been in spinning aircraft twice before and both times had been pinned by the centrifugal force, unable to even lift an arm to move. The first time had in training, as a deliberate exercise so they'd know what to expect, where the aircraft could and was recovered. The second was in C-Charlie which he'd survived only by the grace of Allah: it had been a miracle.

There would be no miracle for the men in the Liberator. If they hadn't already got out already then it was too late.

He turned away, unable to look any more.

Dag, however, was transfixed. Faz could see he was watching them all the way down. How could he do that?

Then Faz got his explanation.

'It's all right, it's going to miss us,' Dag said.

'Vot about ze bombs?' said Marie-Claire.

'They'll land miles away in the direction the Liberator was flying,' Dag reassured her.

Now Faz looked again. The Liberator had gone, as had the formation it had fallen from. All that was left was the contrails of the survivors and some oily smoke from the one that had fallen.

He realised that he'd not even heard it crash. That felt wrong somehow, ten lives had been snuffed out, violently ended, but he'd not heard even a murmur above the crash of the eighty-eights and the sound of the fighting on the beaches. Ten lives, ten families who'd get telegrams in the days and weeks ahead somewhere to the west over the ocean, on a prairie farm, a New York tenement, a Californian orangery, who knew where?

He swallowed, thinking of his wife.

He *would* get back. There would be no telegram.

'All right,' he said. 'How do we get past that battery?'

0840 HOURS
6TH JUNE 1944

'So how did you get past it?'

Faz looked grim. 'With help from above,' he said.

***

'Wait!'

Dag put his hand up to stop them. They'd been creeping up the side of the hedgerow opposite the battery for a good fifteen minutes now, the voices of the German's getting more distinct. Faz judged that they were no more than 50 yards from the battery.

He could see the problem. There was a gap in the hedge, the remains of a gate lay rotting in the long grass. If they crossed over they would, for the first time, be visible from the troops manning the guns.

'What now?' whispered Jones.

'I don't know,' Dag whispered back. He peered around the hedge, cautiously edging further. Then, abruptly, he pulled back.

'They've got guards at the entrance,' he said. 'They don't look too alert but they are so close they can't miss us.'

Faz caught a whiff of tobacco smoke. He guessed the guards were having a cigarette after the action. They were obviously awake and aware of the size of the action that was building all around them. That would mean they'd be on edge, ready to react to any threat they might see, real or imagined. Three men in RAF uniform and a teenage girl still with the remains of her black-up face evident despite her having done her best to wash it off, would definitely be enough. They'd shoot first too.

'Damn it,' whispered Dag. He looked across the field. 'I suppose if we double back and get further in there's a chance we could cross without being seen.' He then looked up. 'Either that or we wait until there's another raid. That would distract them.'

'Bloody Hell, Dag, that's a bit mercenary,' whispered Faz.

'He's right though,' murmured Jones also looking at the skies. 'There's some over there.' He pointed.

Dag shielded his eyes. 'Stirlings I think. Towing gliders. Too far away though.' He looked back towards the battery. 'Those boys will be watching them though. Looking our way, sod them.'

'I could try and distract zem,' said Marie-Claire. 'Ze are men, after all.'

'No!' Dag shook his head. 'Absolutely not.'

'I am a fighter, Zer is no need to protect me,' Marie-Claire was frowning. 'I know you want to get your friend home. I can help.'

'I know,' said Dag. 'But we should stay together. For now, anyway.' He looked at the Stirlings who were now releasing their gliders and banking away to the east rather than towards the battery. 'They may have been warned about it by the Yanks, told to steer clear. Right then, we might as well - what the...?'

Faz knew why he'd stopped talking. Four black dots could be seen low down, hurtling towards them. They were joined by more, a lot more. The shapes resolved into aircraft. Lights twinkled on front of their wings. Faz watched them in fascination until Dag screamed.

'Get down, get down now!'

He dragged Faz down and pulled Marie-Claire to the ground too, then landed on top of both.

Faz's senses, face down as he was in the lush, damp grass, were bombarded by the aroma of the rich earth mixed with the distinct smell of cordite as metal whistled over his head and his ears were assailed with the roar of engines, the whistle of bombs and explosions.

Then thuds started all around him as debris, natural,

man-made and human alike, rained down.

***

'Thunderbolts?' asked Bette.

Faz shook his head. 'Typhoons. The RAF. They came in first with bombs and cannons and then rockets. I guess the Yanks called them in.' He got up and went to stare out of the window. 'It seemed to go on for ever but in fact it was probably over in a minute, maybe a minute and a half at most. They wiped the battery off the map. I've never seen anything like it,' he murmured. 'And never want to see it again as long as I live.

***

Faz's ears were ringing. He was also shaking.

Dag's weight lifted off him. Faz and Marie-Claire gingerly sat up. Faz saw Jones doing the same.

'Everyone all right?' Dag said.

They all nodded, perhaps too stunned to speak. Dag dusted himself down and tried to shake the dirt out of his hair. They all needed to.

All of them and the field around them were covered in earth, and, to Faz's shock, not just earth. There were limbs, bits of uniform, a boot with a lower leg still in it, the shin bone stark white. By his hand was a finger, a ring still on it.

Even with his medical training he felt sick.

'Let's get out of here,' he muttered.

'Come on then,' said Dag.

They moved up to the gap in the hedge. Dag Peered around it again. 'It's clear,' he said.

'God.'

'What is it?' Faz asked.

'Nothing,' Dag muttered. He turned to Marie-Claire. 'Don't look,' he said and tried to guide he beyond the gap. She did, of course, look.

'Mon Dieu,' she said.

Faz could now see what Dag had seen and tried to shield Marie-Claire from. Not the battery, or rather the place where the battery had been, which was a churned-up mess, cratered, with the once mighty 88mm guns ripped apart, fires burning,

113

bodies strewn everywhere. No, the shocking sight was the gunner who'd been flung onto the road, the explosion, either from rocket or bomb having ripped his legs off above the knee. He was crawling towards the battery leaving a trail of blood behind him.

Before Faz knew it he was limping towards the man.

'Faz, come back,' hissed Dag. 'What are you doing?' Faz ignored him. He was kneeling down beside the gunner. He rolled him over. 'My God.'

The gunner was a youth. He looked like he should be in school, his blond hair long and filled with dust.

'Bitte, bitte,' he moaned.

'Keep still, old chap, let's stop that bleeding,' Faz said, not knowing whether the boy could understand him. He took off his belt and looped it round one of the stumps pulling it tight. That still left the other leg. He looked desperately to his companions, still stood in the opening, 'One of you. I need a belt to make a tourniquet. Quickly!'

To his surprise it was Marie-Claire who reacted first. She hurried over, at the same time pulling off her belt. She handed it to Faz. 'What should I do?'

'Keep him calm.' The boy had started to panic, probably having recognised Faz's uniform, He tried to sit up; to pull away, kicking out with his stump as he would have done if his leg was still there. It made Faz's task impossible as well as increasing the blood loss. Marie-Claire knelt behind him and held him. She murmured something to the boy and stroked his hair. The impact on him was immediate, He stopped fighting and stared up at the French girl in wonder. 'Bist du ein Engel?.'

Faz was able to complete his task pulling the belt tight. 'Well done,' he said to Marie-Claire.

She nodded. Faz saw a tear roll down her cheek. Then her eyes widened in horror.

'Faz! look out.'

Dag's shout made Faz look over his shoulder. A pair of German soldiers were advancing from the remains of the battery. One was armed with a machine pistol which he levelled at Faz and Marie-Claire. 'Stop! Halt!' Dag and Jones stepped out levelling their revolvers at the Germans. Time seemed to stop. To Faz it was as if the war was being played out in this one tableau: two opposing armed forces facing each other whilst the youth of the nations lay crying and bleeding in the dirt. Would any of them survive?

It was Marie-Claire who intervened. 'Put your guns down, all of you; she said in English then, in German and directing her words at the soldiers, snapped. 'Can't you see we are trying to save this boy's life. Put your damned guns down and help us.'

***

Bette frowned. 'So what happened?'

Faz smiled.

'Amazingly enough, they did as she said. The next thing I knew the six of us were gathered around this lad trying to save his life. One of them had a first aid kit. He had morphine which we gave the boy as well as sulphur powder and bandages. We spent the next ten minutes cleaning him up and trying to stabilise him.' He looked grim. 'Then we heard the sound of engines.'

***

'There's something coming, sounds like a convoy,' said Jones, looking down the road. 'They' re not far off. Are you done?' Faz nodded. He looked at the Germans who'd been helping him and then down the road. The Germans exchanged glances. One of them stood up.

'You go,' he said, 'Quickly.'

Faz, Marie-Claire, Dag and Jones needed no second invitation, 'thinks. Darke,' said Day.

The German nodded. 'Schnell, Schnell.'

***

'We did 'Schnell:' said Faz. 'By the time the convoy arrived we were well on our way again, in the fields keeping well off the road.'

'Did you make it to the coast?'

'Eventually, yes.'

1120 HOURS
6TH JUNE 1944

Faz, Marie-Claire and Jones huddled behind the shelter they'd found near a tumbledown wall in a derelict farm building.

The noise around them was incredible, shells landing and exploding in a near continuous flow of iron, aircraft roared overhead the chatter of machine guns, rifle's cracking, the staccato bark of the German MG42, a captured example Faz had seen demonstrated during training and had vowed to try to never experience in real life. The air was filled with the scents of war: cordite, smoke — oil and wood smoke alike —, the fresh aroma of churned up earth intermingling with the stink of latrines. Faz was sure there would be many bowels on both sides involuntarily emptied today.

There was a clatter of loose stones, making them all jump. Faz gripped his revolver hard, but it was just Dag, who had gone ahead to scout out the way to the beaches, coming back. His face was grim. 'It's a mess down there,' he said. 'The tide's in and the sea's full of bodies. It's quite a sight, everywhere you look are boats and ships as far as the eye can see.' The ground shook as three huge shells arrived close by. All of them instinctively ducked. 'That's the battleships, at least I assume they're battleships, they're big buggers anyway standing off a few miles from the coast. There's a couple of destroyers cruising in much closer using their guns to bombard the strong points. I saw one blown to bits.'

Dag slumped down.

'Is the invasion succeeding?' asked Jones.

Dag just shrugged. 'I don't know. I just don't know. I can't see how it can't with that amount of firepower, but the defenders are well dug in and firing back. But there's one thing I know for sure: There's no way we can cross that at the moment.'

'We wait then?' said Faz. 'Hope that the invasion succeeds and the troop break out?'

'It's all we can do.' Dag yawned. 'I don't know about you, but I could do with some sleep. I'm all in.'

Faz nodded, though he could see how anyone could sleep through this. 'I'll take first watch,' he said. There was no argument from the other three who settled down to rest. Faz moved to the edge of the building so he could see around the wall. He couldn't see much beyond other than the neighbouring field, a strongpoint a few hundred yards away and a little glimpse of the see but it was as Dag had described: a scene from Dante's Inferno. He wondered how long they'd have to wait.

***

'So how long did you wait?' asked Bette.

'Until it got dark. There were a few alarms, some Jerry troops passed by a few yards away, pulling back from the fighting. luckily, they didn't see us.'

'Did the others sleep?'

'Dag and Jones did. Marie-Claire wasn't able to. Maybe it was because she was younger, who knows? Whatever, we had a long talk, the first we'd managed since we'd met up.'

***

Faz heard a noise and saw Marie-Claire come over to him. She looked pensive.

'I can take over?' she said.

'I'm all right. But feel free to watch with me.'

Oui.' She reached into her pack and took out a canteen. 'I

117

'av water monsieur'

'Thank you,' Faz took a sip. 'Are you all right, Marie-Claire. How are you doing?'

She shrugged. 'I am all right.'

'Are you sure?'

'I am worried. I do not know what will happen to my papa.'

'Your papa? He wasn't at the farm?'

'Non. Zat is why I was with my Grand-père and Grand-mère.'

'Right. Where is he?'

'The Boche took him. He is, 'ow you say, slave worker?'

'He's working for the Germans? In France or Germany?'

'I do not know. But, with vat happened at ze farm...' she shook her head. 'Zey vill know now I am resistance. Vill zey punish him? What have I done?'

'You've done what any patriotic Frenchwoman would have done.' Faz and Marie-Claire looked across at Dag who'd rolled over and was looking at them. 'You fought. He'd be proud of you.'

'Maybe zo but I have decided: I must return, I must find my group. Zey will tell me what to do. They may be able to help my papa.'

Faz frowned. 'You're not coming with us? If we get to England now you can always ask the Allies to send you back.'

Marie-Claire shook her head. 'No, France is my country. I will not leave it. I vill go, once you are safe.'

Both Faz and Dag stared at her in disbelief.

'But you'll be on your own,' Dag said.

'Marie-Claire shrugged. 'Oui. Eet is what eet is, non?'

'But—'

'You could go with her Dag,' Faz interrupted. Both Marie-Claire and Dag stared at him. Jones too had rolled over and blinked at them through sleep clouded eyes.

'Me? But I have to see you home.'

'Do you? I'm here now, aren't I? You've done what you set out to do, or at least you will when the breakout comes.'

Dag stared at him. 'No. I have to go back.'

'Why?' said Faz. 'Back to what? You know what's waiting

for you if you do. So why do it?'

Jones frowned, as did Marie-Claire.

'Facing what?' Jones said. 'What's he talking about, Dag?'

Faz hesitated. He was tired and had gone too far. 'Nothing.'

'Well, it didn't sound like nothing. what's he talking about? What have you done, Dag?'

'You know what I mean. Mac is going to report him for executing that prisoner,' said Faz quickly, not wanting to mention the real reason: LMF.

'What? That was justified. I'll back you up, boyo. The bastard had it coming.'

'Thanks, Jonesy, but that's not what Faz was talking about,' Dag said.

'It was,' Faz protested. 'Dag, don't do it.'

'Don't do what?' demanded Jones.

'Don't tell you that in February I was declared LMF,' said Dag. 'They demoted me. I was left spud bashing until a few months ago.'

Jonesy looked astonished. 'LMF? But...'

'But there's no way back from it. Yes, you're right. Normally. But I have a relative in high places. He pulled strings. Sure, I shouldn't have gone along with it, it was bound to go wrong and it has. It was just a matter of time before they found out.'

'Which is why you shouldn't go back, Dag. Go with Marie-Claire. Help her get back and then just vanish in France. You deserve it. You've done your bit.' Faz grabbed Dag's arm. 'Please Dag.'

Dag shook his head. 'No. I'm going. It's what I deserve. I'm tired. I've had enough. just let it happen.'

***

Bette got to her feet. 'You! You told him to run. You told him not to come back. How could you?'

'I could because he was my friend. He'd done everything to try and get me home. You know it was totally unfair what had happened to him. It seemed the obvious thing to do.' Faz grimaced.

'And he did stay, didn't he? He's alive, isn't he?'

Faz met her gaze. This time he didn't look away. For the first time she doubted herself, doubted John Hinton, doubted even the evidence her own eyes had seen. She'd thought Faz's demeanour since she'd been with him had been down to his knowledge that Dag was alive but now, she saw a different explanation: Faz's guilt was that he couldn't persuade Dag to go. Dag's stubborness had won again.

His next words confirmed it.

'I failed. Dag didn't go along with it. He insisted on going on.' He paused. 'And it killed him.'

LEICESTER
MARCH 1951

'We've reached the end. You know that?' said Faz. 'So do you really want to hear it all?'

'That's what I came for,' said Bette. 'Why stop now?'

'Because I'd rather not relive it, if you don't mind. It wasn't very pleasant. Dag was my friend. It was hard to say goodbye to him then and it hasn't got easier with the passage of time.' He puffed out his cheeks. 'But you don't care, do you? You're going to make me do it anyway.'

Bette couldn't hide her surprise. 'Make you? You're a grown man, Faz, a doctor. You're not in the service so I can't order you to do anything, can I?'

Faz shook his head. 'No, but you'll make me feel obliged to.'

Bette shrugged. 'Possibly. Anyway, we've come this far so you might as well.'

Faz nodded. 'All right. Let's get it over with so I can get back to my family,' He sat back in his chair. 'At somewhere between six and seven in the evening we saw signs that the Americans were getting off the beach and that the fighting was heading in our direction. And then we realised we had a problem.'

1906 HOURS
6TH JUNE 1944

'Somethings happening,' said Dag. He was peering around the wall of their' shelter'. 'The Jerries are withdrawing. It looks like the Yanks have made it to the top of the bluff'.

Faz joined Dag at his viewpoint. Sure enough, grey-clad figures could be seen, running, ducking down, firing behind them. And there, for the first time, there were glimpse of green uniformed US GIs, moving up, taking positions, fighting to clear the ground. They were making good progress, working in teams, covering each other.

'Good lads, that's it,' Dag muttered. 'Oh God, get back, quickly.'

Faz could see what Dag had seen. A group of the Germans were heading right towards them.

'They want this as a strong point,' he muttered, pulling out his revolver. Faz did the same. They watch the German troops carefully, ready to shoot if they got too close

Luckily, at the last minute, they veered off to one side, the other side of the wall that the Jones and Marie-Claire sheltered.

'Fuck!' Dag cursed and he and Faz hurried to join the other two, Dag holding up his fingers to his mouth.

'What is it?' whispered Jones.

'Some Jerries,' whispered Faz, 'They've taken up a position just next to us.'

Voices could now be heard on the other side of the wall, audible despite the racket that still continued outside.

Then the unmistakable bark of an MG42 started.

'That's not good,' said Jones.

Screams and shouts could be heard from where Faz had seen the GIs.

'They're picking off the Yanks, damn them.'

'For now, yes, but they won't get away with it for long. Those boys are hard. They've got grenades and bazookas,' said Dag. 'I don't fancy getting in the way of those Yanks with their blood up.'

'They could call in the navy guns too,' observed Faz.

'What do we do? Run? Out there?' Jones pointed at the bluff. 'See if we can get the Yanks to see us?'

'I don't fancy that,' said Faz.

Bullets started to ping off the wall in front of them.

'We can't stay here. We've got to do something. *I've* got to do something.'

Dag, crouching, crept towards the end of the wall.

'Where are you going?' Faz whispered urgently. Dag didn't answer. But Faz realised, to his horror, what Dag's goal was.

***

'He attacked the German's?' said Bette. 'Single-handed?'

'At first. Then Jones joined in. It was chaos. The shooting went on and on.'

'How did it end?'

***

Faz tried to move, tried to help Jones and Dag but he and Marie-Claire were pinned down by bullets coming in from all around them. It seemed that all the small arms in Normandy were, at that moment, aimed at them. Faz wanted to it to stop, wanted to wave a white flag, to scream for help but he and the French girl could do nothing but cower in the dirt waiting for the end, waiting for the moment when the lead ripped into them.

Then, abruptly, a wave of heat swept over them.

All went black.

***

'Whether it was a grenade, or a mortar or even a shell from the ships, I've no idea. Whatever, the wall we were sheltering behind collapsed onto us. I was knocked out, pinned down. I'd probably be there now if it wasn't for Marie-Claire. She'd missed the worst of the blast and the wall, freed herself then tried to dig me out with her bare hands. Luckily, the Yanks spotted her and, because she was a woman, held their fire. I came to to the sound of American voices.'

'The GIs arrived and helped to dig you out?'

Faz nodded. 'They did. Luckily for us the Germans had been killed by the blast, and the top of that bluff had been just about cleared.' He closed his eyes for a moment. 'Of course, the Germans were not the only ones on that side of the wall.' Faz opened his eyes again an stared at Bette. 'So that was the end. That's the story. That was where Dag died. Fighting to save my life.'

LEICESTER
MARCH 1951

'They were dead. All of them?' She actually knew the answer but asked the question, nonetheless.

'Dag was. I thought Jones was too, but he started groaning. His face was pretty lacerated by the shrapnel, and he'd got a fair bit of the same in his chest. The Yanks called in one of their medics and managed to staunch the bleeding.'

Bette swallowed. Her throat was suddenly very dry.

'Dag was beyond help?' she managed to force out the words.

'Yes, he was.' Faz shook his head. 'He was a mess. I'm not going to go into details so don't ask me. The effect of high explosives and metal on the human body have to be seen to be believed. I saw it once, I'd rather not even think about it again, if you don't mind.'

Bette nodded. She looked down at the envelope she still held. She had her answer.

'Yes, that's fine,' she said. 'It must have been hard for you. Then and now.'

'It was. I was bereft. In shock. I couldn't believe it. He'd got so close, got me to the Americans but couldn't get to freedom himself.' Faz stopped speaking. He stared at Bette. 'But then I remembered what Dag would have faced if he had got back. Mac would have made his report about the execution, and, in any case, Dag knew that the cat would have been let out of the bag about him being LMF. He'd have gone through the shame all over again. It wasn't right. It wasn't fair.' Faz's gaze became even fiercer. 'It was for the best he died then and there.

I'm sorry, but that's the truth.'

Bette and Faz stared at each other for a few seconds. Then she broke the eye-contact and looked down at the envelope she still clutched. When she looked up, she saw that Faz was also looking at it.

Abruptly she rose. She held out her hand.

'Thank you, Faz,' she said. 'That's put my mind at rest. Squadron-leader Hinton was obviously mistaken.'

Faz nodded. He smiled.

'Thank-you, Bette,' he said.

They shook hands.

'Mac didn't get back, did he? At least not straight away?'

'No, he was caught with the two Yanks a few hours after we left. He ended up in a POW camp. He didn't get home until after VE day.'

She nodded. She was about to leave but there was one last question she needed to ask.

'The girl. Marie-Claire. What happened to her?'

'She came back with us. The Americans wouldn't let her stay in France like she wanted. She argued for a while but, in the end, I think she saw the sense in going to England. As it was it took weeks for her farm to be liberated. She helped treat Jones and rode back with us on an LST when the wounded were evacuated.'

Bette thought about this for a few moments. 'And afterwards?

'She went back to France, I suppose.'

'Didn't you keep in touch?'

A faint smile told Bette all she needed to know.

A few minutes later Bette was back in her car. She placed the envelope on the seat next to her. She looked at it for a moment then opened it and took out the photograph. It was taken at Gatow in Germany in early 1949. A clear picture of a pilot striding out to his Dakota. He had changed, he was scarred and had filled out a bit, but he was still recognisable. She smiled, nodded to herself, put the photograph back in the enveloped and started the engine.

It was time to get back to her life.

***

Faz stood at the window of his office and watched her drive away. Once he was satisfied she had gone he went back and looked at the photograph of the Halifax and thought about that evening of the 6th June 1944 in Normandy.

The evening when Dag ceased to be.

***

Faz watched as the medic worked to band up the blood-soaked figure on the grand. The patient, despite his wounds, made no complaint, partly because his injuries included damage to his mouth and jaw but mainly, Faz assumed, of who he was. He just stoically accepted his treatment just as he always seemed to accept everthing else that had happened to him. His only concession was to hold the hand of Marie-Claire, kneeling next to him.

Faz looked across to the bodies laid out by the wall. They were all mutilated, limbs either missing or hanging on by a thread. Two in field-grey, one in RAF blue. Faz shook his head, his erstwhile companion had been eviscerated and all but been decapitated. He was unrecognisable.

The medic stood up. 'He'll do for now,' he said. 'I've radioed down to the beach, they know where you are. They'll come and get you.'

'Thanks,' said Faz. 'Do you think he'll be all right?

The medic looked at the prone figure. 'Yeah, I reckon so. He's skinny but tough.' He looked across the top of the bluff as the sound of gunfire increased. 'I'd better catch up with the boys. Look after yourself, bud.'

'You too, soldier.'

The American shook Faz's hand, nodded at Marie-Claire. 'Madam', then hurried off.

'Vat now?' said Marie-Claire. 'What vill happen to 'im ven ve get to Angletairre?'

'He'll be disgraced. Face court-martial probably.'

'Vy? why do that?'

'The RAF demoted him. They say he's a coward.'

'Zat is unfair. He is, 'ow you say, hero.'

Faz nodded. 'It is. He shouldn't go home. Remember I tried to persuade him not to.'

He looked at Dag then at the body of Jones. He smiled. 'Maybe Dag doesn't have to go home.'

He saw Marie-Claire frown but didn't explain. Instead, he lent over Dag, reaching under his uniform for his dog tags. He saw Dag look puzzled, then, as he pulled the dog tags off over Dag's head, saw him weakly shake his head.

Faz ignored him, He went over to Jones, steeling himself for what he was about to do. 'Excuse me, old chap. You don't mind, do you?' He found it easier than he thought. Within moments he'd exchanged Jones' dog tags for Dag's. Marie-Claire was watching him. She nodded. She'd understood. Still, she frowned.

'Vat about zis man's relatives?'

'He had no one close. He told me that. There's no one waiting for him.'

'Vill Dag go along with it?'

Faz shrugged. 'He's as stubborn as a mule normally but now I'm safe and with the right persuasion, maybe.'

'Oui. Je suis, d'accord. Do it quickly.' she looked across the top of the bluff. 'Someone is coming.'

'Dag. Understand. This is what's happening. This is for the best. Just accept it. Yes?' Faz said as he put the dog tags round Dag's neck.

This time Dag did not protest. In fact, Faz was sure there was a ghost of a smile from beneath the bandages.

'Good luck, Daffyd,' murmured Faz. He looked at Jones' body. 'Rest in peace, Dag.'

POSTSCRIPT: NORMANDY JUNE 1952

Bette sipped her lemonade and watched from the cover of the cafes umbrella as the woman, holding the hand of a small boy, possibly three or four years' old, whilst pushing a pram with the other hand as they strolled from the bakery to the greengrocer.

The boy was doing what most boys of his age, from Bette's observations at least, swinging from his mother's arm, trying to pull away then falling behind, almost being pulled over. His mother, though with the added burden of the pram, was unconcerned and relaxed.

Bette scrutinised her carefully from behind her sunglasses. The woman strolled with a languid, long-limbed ease, her slim frame enhanced a simple blue polka-dot cotton dress that, on her, could have come from a Paris fashion house instead, as Bette suspected, being hand made on the woman's sewing machine.

Of course she'd be attractive, and had shrugged off the effects of two pregnancies and labours with a relaxed ease, of course she'd be talented with a needle. Bette tried not to be jealous, but she accepted that she was not going to succeed. She'd become accustomed to accepting. Her favourite saying was now 'Beggars can't be choosers.'

It was not the first time she had seen the woman. The

first time had been an accident, at the farm. Bette had not expected the encounter. She'd taken a taxi from the closest town just out of curiosity. She'd stood at the top of the lane that led to the farm buildings, the taxi waiting for her, the driver showing no curiosity.

The woman had appeared out of the blue, driving a small herd of cows to milking, she'd frowned as she passed Bette in the lane. The woman was dressed in a pair of overalls a couple of sizes too big; she looked ridiculously young. Heart pounding, Bette had got back in the taxi and hurried back to town.

She should have moved on. Should have gone to visit the cemetery in Bayeux to honour a few old friends but found herself booking into the town's one hotel, in the certain knowledge that, in the, the woman would likely come there shopping. She had. Twice. The first time alone, the second time was now, with her children this time. What did Bette hope to achieve? This was pointless, something that she'd resisted doing for a year and a quarter, she'd known it was a silly thing to do but she had to know. Well, now she did: Time to move on. She finished her lemonade and looked for the waiter to get the bill.

'Bonjour, Madame.' Bette had not seen the woman approach.

'Hello... er...Bon après-midi.'

'We should speak English, no? Your accent is terrible.'

The woman sat down without being invited.

'I'm sorry,' said Bette, though what she had to apologise about she didn't know.

'Why apologise?' The woman waved at the waiter. 'Une carafe de vin rouge, s'il vous plaît et deux verres.' she said, then turned to Bette. 'You were at my farm, yes?'

Bette never thought about lying.

'Yes, I was. Sorry, I didn't want you to think I was spying on you.'

'Except you were, no?'

Bette nodded. 'I suppose so. Where are your children?'

'With their grand pere. He is also in town.'

'I see.'

'He doesn't want me talking to you. He thinks it is

unwise.'

Bette smiled. 'Why is that Marie-Claire?'

The waiter brought the carafe of wine and two glasses before Marie-Claire could reply. Instead, she poured some into both before Bette could protest that she didn't actually care for wine. She had no choice but to accept it. She took a sip. To her surprise it was much more pleasant than the near vinegar she'd previously tried.

'You know who I am?' said Marie-Claire. 'So, I presume you are Madame Baxter?'

'Faz has been busy I see,' Bette muttered. Then she nodded, 'Yes, I am, Madame Jones. I presume that is your married name?'

Marie-Claire nodded 'Oui. What of it? What is it you want? why have you come here?'

Bette had to admire her directness. Now she had to answer the question she, herself had been asking.

'I don't know.' Bette held up her hands. 'I simply don't know. I was just curious, I suppose.'

'About what? Dr Khan said that it was clear you knew he was alive.'

'I do, yes.'

'Then what? To expose him? Others have tried.'

'But have been shut down by a certain retired Air-Commodore who pulled strings to have his file made secret for 50 years? Don't worry, revealing who he is is the last thing I want to do.'

'Then what do you want? Why are you spying on us?'

Bette drew breath. She'd asked herself this so often.

'I just wanted to know if he was happy. That you are happy. Are you?' Then she shook her head. 'I didn't need to ask, did I? You are and he is, isn't he? He's happy and content and a great father to boot, yes?'

Marie-Claire looked like she was going to react angrily but, abruptly, she relaxed, she laughed. 'Oui. He is and I am. I didn't think I was the type to be a wife and mother but, oui, that's what I am and he makes it easy.'

Bette smiled. 'Good. Is he flying at the moment?'

'Yes, he is. He is on a freight flight to Belgium. He is

coming back tonight though. It is the commemoration at the weekend. Would you like to come home with me? See him?'

Bette shook her head. 'No. I don't. Not that I wouldn't like to see him it's just, well, it would hurt. I guess I'm a coward.'

Marie-Claire raised her eyebrows in amusement. 'Eet is perhaps a good thing that the RAF has got rid of LMF, no?'

Bette nodded. 'Yes, absolutely. I would be convicted.' She drained her wineglass. 'Tell him I'm happy for him. And for you too. I must go.'

'Where to? Home?'

'Yes, but I've got one last thing to do before I go.'

'What is that?'

'I have to pay a visit to a certain grave in Bayeux. I think you know whose?'

Marie-Claire nodded 'Give Atkinson-Grieve my regards,' she said.

'I will,' said Bette. 'And I'm going to put this on it and give thanks.'

She opened her handbag and took out a piece of cloth, carefully folded. Bette unfolded it and showed it to Marie-Claire.

It was a Welsh flag.

Marie-Claire smiled and nodded.

'Oui,' she said. 'Thank him for me too.'

THE END

AFTERWORD

I hope you enjoyed Last Man Home.

The **LMF trilogy** is now complete, Dag has a completed story arc.

You should note that **LMF** was never intended to be part of a series. It was a standalone novel that was meant to both tell the story of one crew, on one night and to explore the rather horrible threat the RAF held over its crews; being declared to 'Lack Moral Fibre' if they turned back or failed to bomb without what was deemed to be a reasonable excuse. Readers seemed to think it did that and I could have left it there.

But there were loose ends, not least of which was what happened to men who were on the receiving end of an LMF finding. As a result I wrote **The Way Back**. That was intended to finish the story.

But, of course, it didn't. I left Dag in France, shattered by finding the graves of his crew who had shown such faith and loyalty to him and whom he thought he'd saved.

More loose ends. I couldn't leave it like that.

Hence **Last Man Home**. Now you know that, whilst Dag never actually did go home, he had a life afterwards, albeit not under his own name.

So that is finally it. Honestly! Unless I find some more loose ends of course.

In the meantime would you do me a great favour? Can you leave a rating and review on either Amazon of Goodreads? It helps me get feedback and other readers to find my books.

Thanks in advance.

Malcolm
September 2025

Printed in Dunstable, United Kingdom